# FINDING BEAUTY Within

## A KALEIDASTORM STORY
## WITH
## JOURNAL PROMPTS

I0662484

# LORI KIRKLAND

**BOOKS BY LORI KIRKLAND**

•Finding Beauty Within (2025)
•Tucked in Flowers (2024)

**Written and published as Lori Minutoli**

•Emotional Bouquet- Filler Flowers (2023)
•Emotional Bouquet- Greenery (2022)
•Emotional Bouquet- Roses (2021)
•Emotional Bouquet- Wildflowers (2020)
•Released To The Wild (2019)
•From My Heart (2018)
•Kaleidastorm (2016)

**Written and published under pen names:**
**Lora Makanani** and HellionSaint

•Poets In Love (2016)


Books available via **lori-kirkland.com**

# Finding Beauty
## *Within*

## Lori Kirkland

lorikirkland

# The Sound of Beauty

*There's no point in getting out of bed*, she thought. Curled up beneath a mound of blankets, on a cart in the basement, she pulled the fleece over her head to contain her body heat. The air in the room was painfully cold on her face. Living in the abandoned house with no heat during the winter months proved to be quite a struggle.

*I have nowhere to go, no one to see, no money, no car, no job, nothing,* she thought.

It was a season of hard times for Ashley. Losing her job and squatting in this house left her feeling completely alone. No one was looking for her, and no one knew she was staying there.

To gain entrance into the house, she cut through the woods long before the property and slipped in through an unlocked back door. She was certain that curious neighbors were unaware of her presence.

Stilling her thoughts once inside, she cleared her mind. Motionless in the bed, her breathing slowed. She lay there without any more thoughts, without emotions, without agitation, simply void of everything but body heat. Dark, quiet, and calm rested with her.

In her mind's eye, from under the covers, she looked out the window towards the woods. Seeing the stark trees in all of their twisted, broken forms caused her to wonder how they had the strength to endure the harsh winters. She imagined the pain they must have suffered from the brutal winds ripping down their branches and heavy snow snapping their limbs. Some entire trees were uprooted, revealing their shallow roots. *Just like me,* she thought.

She saw the invasive wisteria and bittersweet vines choking out the life of some branches, twisting and circling the trees from base to top, then reaching across to other trees. Ashley knew the feeling of life being choked out of her as well.

Bringing her thoughts back inside, under the covers, she roamed through the darkness of her mind, searching for something to spark an internal fire, something to cause an excitement that would make her want to get out of bed. She roamed the hallways of her mind, looking everywhere.

As she passed each room, she took note of what was there. *Love used to be in here, but now it's dead.*

*Interests used to be in this room, but now there are none. Hobbies in here, now gone. Friends—all gone, pets—all dead, family—all gone, childhood memories were in one room, but they caused nothing but misery, so those memories are also now gone. Is there anything in this darkness? Anything?* Ashley challenged her thoughts.

Opening her eyes and removing the covers from her face, she looked around to see if she was still alive or possibly dreaming. It was such a strange place to be— in the dark without emotions. Looking around the room didn't change anything. Ashley felt dead. The sting in her nose from the cold air, however, told her she was, in fact, still alive.

Back under the fleece blankets, she talked to herself. Mustering up a little bit of frustration, she screamed, "*I just want to feel something*!" followed by "*AAAAAAHHHHHH!*"

Nothing. She felt nothing. *Maybe I'll think of something sad*.

Ashley recalled tragedies she'd seen on the news, thought of starving children in war-torn countries, she even recollected the image of her parents laid out in coffins, but nothing moved her enough to get emotional. She acknowledged that her heart was cold, black, and simply void of everything. *I must be dead*, she thought as she drifted off to sleep.

The afternoon sun warmed the basement room. Startled upon waking, she flew off the covers in need of air. The sun was beating on the pile of blankets, and she was sweltering under them. Now awake, nature called. She grabbed her iPod and headed to the bathroom.

After seeing her disheveled self in the mirror, she deemed a shower necessary. Stepping into the hot water, she robotically cleaned her body. Even that did not trigger a reaction, no soothing emotions, no pleasure, no happiness; she just washed up and got out.

Once in sweats and a hoodie, she grabbed her iPod and curled up in the overstuffed chair near the window. Her playlist had been updated while at the library the day before. Noticing a new album, she popped the earbuds in each ear and pulled her hood over her head.

Gazing out the window, looking at the cold, lifeless, broken trees was like looking in the mirror to her. With her head hung to one side and resting on her arms atop pulled-up knees, she pressed play.

As soon as the music began, her head perked up, her eyes opened wider, and her brain registered the sensation now vibrating through her nerves. The guttural sound of the singer's voice instantly sent a ripple from her ears through her entire body. As he sang deep vibratos, her mind went into spasms, her shoulders rose to embrace her ears to calm the tingling sensations.

Unable to stand it any longer, she pulled both earbuds out with one tug of the cord. Rubbing her ears and then her head with both hands, Ashley was stunned at what had just happened. Her eyes bounced around as she tried to comprehend it.

"That was amazing!" she declared as a rush of excitement coursed through her veins.

Smiling and now curious to see if it would happen again, she put the earbuds back in. There was a different song playing. This one had a delicate guitar melody. It was soft and pretty. She closed her eyes and let her head sway to the soothing sound.

Then he sang a tender melody, yet there was pain in his tone. Sensing anguish in his voice and the lyrics, her eyes tightened, and her heart began to ache. He was singing, but it almost sounded like he was crying as he sang the lyrics. Tears fell from her eyes onto her arm, which caught her by surprise. She hadn't realized she was crying.

Once again, she yanked the earbuds out, wiped her eyes, and squeezed her forehead with her left hand, trying to shake off the strange feelings she was experiencing. She looked at her iPod to see who the artist was, but didn't recognize his name. Telling herself she must have pre-ordered the album a while ago, she looked and saw there were eight more songs. She was now more curious than ever. Ashley was unaware of the numbness in her fingers or the fact that her breath could be seen when she exhaled. All she was focused on was the power of this music and the variety of feelings now overtaking her entire being.

Again, the earbuds went back in. This time, she heard him singing a slightly familiar song. She bobbed her head up and down as it played. She remembered hearing this song and ordering the album back when she still had a job. This song spoke of the injustice in the world. It was an angry kind of song, one she could relate to. It reminded her why she was so numb, cold, and heartless. It reminded her of why she could connect with the dead-looking trees outside.

Without noticing that the song changed, suddenly a shiver raced down her spine and tingled the roots of every hair on her head. Shaking it off, she forced herself to listen to every word. The lyrics told a story. He loved someone. He was singing about all the ways he enjoyed her. At one point, Ashley's eyebrows raised as the words described something she wasn't familiar with—passion. She had never known passion like he was singing about. The song ended with "I'm gonna love you forever."

On that note, she pressed stop and turned off the iPod. Removing the earbuds one at a time, she laid them in her lap and began daydreaming about love. She had never been in love. She couldn't recall being loved, even by her parents. She replayed the lyrics over and over in her mind to trying to understand. She wondered for a moment if she could be loved and desired, like the girl in the song.

With fire racing through her blood, she felt her cheeks flush at the thought of being desired. A shiver woke her from the daydream to the reality that she was freezing. She couldn't feel her fingers or her nose, so she climbed back under the blankets and shivered, waiting for the heat to collect. She breathed into her hands and rubbed them together, desperate for relief. The sting was harsh, but her mind was filled with new thoughts, enough to keep her warm, at least in her mind.

As she rewound the music in her mind, she recalled the excitement, the sadness, the burning in her veins of desire, and then it hit her—she wasn't in the void anymore. She was feeling very much alive. She had experienced feelings, and they felt good.

As she thought about the girl he sang about, she drifted off to sleep feeling embraced by all of these new sensations.

# The Dream

Buried beneath a mound of blankets, Ashley fought demons in the dark. With tension in her face along with the grunts that escaped her tight lips as she flailed against her bed, she grasped her sheets while digging her heels into the mattress.  She was fighting against something terrifying. Something was definitely after her or maybe even had her in its clutches.

A shrill rang out and woke Ashley. It was her scream that she heard. Gasping for air and dotting her eyes around the room, she lay there for a moment until she realized she wasn't in her nightmare any longer. The warmth of her body comforted her as she recalled being chased through the snowy woods, falling down an embankment, and grabbing hold of a small tree, which kept her from plummeting to the icy river below.

Rubbing her hands along the length of her arms and wrapping herself in an embrace, she closed her eyes and calmed her breathing. *I'm okay. It was only a dream,* she assured herself.

Once settled, Ashley sat up, swung her feet over the bed, and into her slippers. She checked her phone for the time and then headed to the kitchen. Along the way, she twisted open the mini blinds and glanced outside. The sun was shining, not a cloud in the sky. In fluid-like motion, she set up the coffee maker, fixed herself a bagel, and filled a tall glass with water. As she stood against the counter in her nightshirt, sipping her coffee, she thought about what she was going to wear today.

Every day, Ashley had the same routine. She made breakfast, packed a healthy lunch, took the train to work, and was back home by dinner time, only to go out again to her second job. At the end of the day, she was so exhausted that she usually just crashed on the couch until she was ready for bed.

Deciding on the red dress and strappy shoes, Ashley was going for the flirty look. She was an introvert mostly, but when it came to dressing up for work, she got a thrill when it came to showing her wild side. It only came out in her wardrobe, though, as her demeanor was polite, professional, and on the quiet side. It created an air of mystery when she wore things contrary to her character, and seeing the expression on people's faces energized her. Even so, she had mastered the art of concealing her excitement when she dressed this way.

Walking to the train, she felt exhilarated. Even though this was the same day she woke from a terrifying dream, she was now renewed in her mind and was in the safety of her familiar surroundings. A smile crossed her face as she thought *Today is gonna be a great day.*

She noticed the colors in people's clothing. Vibrant colors also dotted the landscape like never before. Was it her attitude? Was it her mindset? Were these colors here every day? Something was different today. Something was in the air.

Once on the train, feeling full of energy, Ashley chose to stand for the ride across town. With an arm around the pole, she put her earbuds in and tuned out the world. The new music stimulated her senses and made her feel very much alive. She would soon be a woman on fire, first with the red dress, then with the tempting music. Of course, she kept all of this deeply hidden as she stood there, motionless with her eyes closed for much of the ride.

When the train stopped to pick up passengers, she opened her eyes and immediately saw him making eye contact with her.

Mr. Handsome hadn't taken his eyes off her from the moment he stepped on the train; he simply backed himself against the cabin wall near the door. She felt the heat rise up her neck, flushed her cheeks, and immediately she looked down at her iPod. It wasn't because he was staring at her, but that she found him very attractive. She hadn't felt that before. Plenty of men looked at her when she walked to work, and she always smiled and looked away. This was different.

As the train continued, she tried to keep her eyes closed and listen to music. She couldn't help but wonder about this tall, blonde, handsome man. She opened her eyes, and immediately her breath hitched as he was once again locking eyes with hers. Fighting the urge to look away, she held her eyes fixed on his. She wondered what he was thinking. Her thoughts were racing as the music played in her ears.

Suddenly, the train jostled, and she lost her footing for a moment. Righting herself against the pole, Ashley decided to take a break from looking at Mr. Handsome. She angled her stance slightly in a different direction and forced herself not to look at him in order to gather her thoughts. *Who is this guy? What is going on here?* She stopped the music so she could think. Looking down with her head slightly tilted, unable to fully comprehend this intense attraction, she decided to put it out of her mind. *I'll just avoid him,* she thought.

As she went to exit the train, Mr. Handsome decided he would as well.

"After you," he said in a deep tone, causing the hairs on the back of her neck to rise.

"Thank you," she said in a barely audible voice. As she passed by him, Ashley noticed and approved of his square-tipped brown leather shoes, slim-fitted khaki slacks, and tailored shirt, taut against his chest. *This guy has style, and does he ever smell amazing..* The spicy scent of his cologne sent her thermostat into the danger zone.

As she walked along the cobblestone sidewalk toward her building, she had the feeling he was behind her, but dared not look back. *I just have to get inside my building,* she thought, then quickened her pace. These extraordinary sensations she was experiencing were beginning to make her feel uncomfortable. It would have been enough to just bask in the thrill of the eye contact on the train, had he not gotten off the same stop she could've dwelled on the intrigue of that alone.

Just as she reached for the door handle, his hand covered hers, and he pulled it open.

"Allow me," he requested, nearly in her ear. Electricity went through her body at the touch of his hand on hers. Looking up at him, into the windows of his soul, she smiled, slipped her hand away, and walked in. *This cannot be happening to me right now.* If this had been any other man extending this courtesy towards her, she would have engaged in friendly conversation. But the sensations she was feeling were too intense to speak through, so she just kept walking.

Thinking she could avoid any further accidental contact with him, Ashley diverted to the stairs instead of the elevator. *It's only six floors.* Being a runner, she would make the hike up the six flights without any trouble, that is, if Mr. Handsome wasn't on her tail, but he was.

While wondering if she should sprint up the stairs to lose him or casually walk up as if she was unaffected by his presence, she slipped on a pencil and fell to her knees.

Swooping her up to her feet, Mr. Handsome did not comment, only kept one hand on her back until she steadied herself. He didn't say anything that would add to her embarrassment. He only smiled and looked deeply into her eyes. She had no choice but to talk to him now.

"Thank you. I'm…" and she lost her words as she felt his hand still on her back.

Noticing her sudden loss of words, he picked up where she left off. "I'm Brad. It seems we're heading in the same direction."

With those words, she snapped out of her trance and said, "It appears so."

She told him her name and proceeded to walk up the stairs. "Sixth floor?" he asked.

Reluctantly, she replied, "Yes."

This time, Ashley waited at the door for Brad to open it. *Avoid contact,* she kept telling herself. Once inside the office, they parted ways. She had no idea who he was or which office he worked in, but for certain, she would see him again.

Once inside her office, she let out a sigh of relief and dropped down in her chair. Spinning around to look out the window, feeling the sun on her face, she closed her eyes and thought about Brad. Drifting off into a daydream, she knew she had indeed felt desired, just like the girl in the song.

KNOCK! KNOCK! KNOCK! The wrapping on the door woke her again. She jumped from the bed, stuck her feet in her boots, grabbed her coat, and went to the door to see who was there. "Who is it?" she nervously asked.

"It's Alice, the neighbor from across the street."

The neighbor sounded like an old lady, so Ashley opened the door. A cold wind rushed past her. Standing there bundled up against the cold, Alice held a basket covered with a dish towel.

"I've seen you coming and going, honey, so I brought you these homemade goodies." She waited for Ashley to take the basket from her trembling hands.

"When you're finished, just leave the basket at my mailbox. I'll see it."

Smiling, she turned and walked away, leaving Ashley holding the basket. When a second wind blew across her face, she hurried to shut the door. Now more confused than ever, she wondered what was real and what was only a dream.

From under the towel, Ashley inhaled the warm apple cinnamon aroma. Taking a muffin and pressing it to her face, she warmed her cheek and inhaled the delicious scent. Then she remembered the dream she had just woken from.

Setting down the basket, taking the muffin over to the chair by the window, she curled up under a blanket. Memories of Brad came back to her mind. *In my dream, I had a life. I had two jobs, an apartment, food, and clothes, and I was happy. I was even desired.* She thought about those things for a long while. She liked Ashley in the dream. As the apple muffin warmed her stomach and her senses, she began to feel something stir inside her.

Not only in her stomach, but in her heart and mind, Ashley began to feel something she hadn't felt in a long time. She felt the desire for more. She was now thinking maybe it was possible to start over, to have a dream and go after it. This was her aha moment when she realized the dream was motivating her to want more out of life. Even though it was only a dream, she had felt the exhilaration of wearing the flirty red dress, she felt the attraction to the handsome man, and she felt his desire for her.

Considering the two dreams she had today, the horrible nightmare, and the exciting dream, Ashley realized she needed to decide what she was going to do with her life. There was no question really, Ashley knew without a doubt that she would start looking for a job right away. *I'm going to believe in my dream.*

Smiling, she let her imagination run wild as the sun shone through the trees and shadows danced on the snow-covered ground outside the window.

# The Plan

Pounding the pavement through the back roads on her evening run, Ashley exercised a mental workout. Having a new found desire to strive for more was exciting but also challenging. She had not yet learned to believe she was worth receiving anything good; she only knew that it was something she wanted. In order to get through tough days, she often remembered how the Ashley in her dream handled things. It was a mind game that worked enough to get her a job and help her communicate with people. By the end of the day, however, self-doubt and a slew of negative thoughts tormented her. Running helped her process these thoughts. As she ran she thought, *I want this now*, *I want to make something of my life! I have nothing left to lose, so it can only get better, right?* Even so, doubt always had a way of sneaking in.

Pressing harder into her run, she pushed herself to fight off the negative thoughts. At times, she felt like she was in a boxing ring. As her arms moved in sync with her stride, she jabbed at the air, knocking each negative attack away. "It's my turn!"

19

she declared with the right jab to a negative thought telling her she wouldn't get the promotion at work.

"I am determined! I am strong! I am confident!"

Ashley gave voice to her self-affirmations. Each one empowered her to believe in herself and what she would accomplish with a positive mindset.

As she turned onto the long road leading to the house, she saw firetrucks and a large crowd of people standing in the street. From afar off, she could see the black smoke billowing above the trees and an orange glow against the evening sky. *Could it be?* she wondered.

Sprinting as fast as she could, she needed to see if it was her house on fire. The moment she realized it was, she stopped in her tracks, clenched her stomach, and keeled over crying. She began to tremble in shock that she no longer had a place to live and that her few belongings were destroyed. It seemed even the forces of nature were against her.

*Where do I go now? Where am I gonna live? What about my work clothes? Oh no… My job!*

Her mind raced as terrifying thoughts consumed every ounce of reason in her. "No… Not now!" she cried out. *Not when I have so much…*

She couldn't even finish her thought. The pressure in her head and the intensity of her sobbing consumed her. Having emotions this powerful was something Ashley wasn't used to. She had suffered so much loss in her life that she had grown cold and heartless. She had been void of emotions to the point where she thought she was dead on the inside. What she felt now was real and it hurt.

When exhausted from crying, she stood upright with one hand on her hip and walked in circles, trying to decide what to do. Wiping her face with her sleeve, she took a deep breath, mustered up enough courage to get closer, and walked the rest of the way. As she got closer, she heard the angry howls of the fire consuming the house and the whistles of the water from the firetrucks as they hosed down the house.

Standing on the backside of the crowd, looking only at the house on fire, she did not notice Alice touching her arm until Alice put both hands around Ashley and hugged her from the side. In that moment, Ashley looked into the loving face of Alice, her neighbor, and instantly broke down crying again. She turned and put her head on Alice's shoulder and wept. Alice just held her and didn't say a word. For nearly an hour, they stood and watched as the fire tore through the house, as the fireman worked to put it out.

Alice noticed that Ashley was shivering and placed one arm through Ashley's and said, "Come with me, dear," and guided her towards the house across the street.

"Oh, Alice, what am I…" as tears begin to fall once again, Ashley couldn't get the words out, but Alice knew what she was trying to say.

"Don't worry, dear, you can stay with me. I have a little room perfect that's for you."

Once inside, Alice showed her the room she had prepared for her. On the foot of the bed was a folded set of pajamas and a towel. She indicated to Ashley that they were for her and suggested she go take a shower.

"You have this ready for me?" Ashley managed to say. "I don't understand."

Alice replied, "You take a shower and I'll fix us some tea. We'll talk when you're done. The bathroom is down the hall on the right."

Still in shock, Ashley simply obeyed the nice woman and took the clean clothes to the bathroom.

Feeling the hot water embrace her cold body, she stood in the shower with her head hung low and silently let the tears fall from her eyes.

When Ashley came out to the kitchen after her shower, Alice had set the table with a meal for both of them. She pulled out a chair for Ashley and then sat across the table. Alice bowed her head, gave thanks for the food, and then lifted the teapot to fill their cups.

"Alice, I don't understand why you had clothes for me."

"Dear, those clothes have been there all winter. I have been waiting for you. I never imagined you would have made it this long in that house."

"How did you know…" Ashley tried to speak.

Interrupting her, Alice said, "Let's eat and talk later."

She lifted the fork to serve a piece of ham to Ashley and then one to herself. Ashley added steamed vegetables and rice to her plate. The two ate in silence, both of their hearts filling along with their stomachs.

Upon finishing the meal, Ashley placed her napkin on the plate, looked up at Alice with a gentle smile, and said, "Thank you." Alice just smiled and nodded her head.

The two cleared the table, washed and dried the dishes together, then sat in the living room. The Old English-style furniture was pretty to look at but somewhat hard to sit on. Ashley guessed that not many people had sat on this furniture. It seemed like it was more for display than comfort. Before sitting down, Alice brought a fleece blanket over to Ashley and said, "Wrap yourself in this and get comfortable."

Alice sat in her Queen Anne chair, put her feet up on the ottoman, and covered herself with a fleece blanket as well. "I'm sorry you lost your belongings, dear."

Trying to keep a positive attitude, something she decided after her shower, Ashley told the woman that not everything was lost. Lifting her sleeve, she showed Alice the arm strap wallet she had on and said, "I still have my ID and my bank card. I take them with me when I run in case anything happens to me."

Realizing the irony in what she just said, Ashley smiled and felt a slight feeling of victory inside her. *All is not lost,* she thought. "I can buy new clothes for work."

"That is wonderful news, dear. I suggest that you look through the closet in the bedroom you're sleeping in tonight. I believe there may be something that fits you in there. Some might even still have tags on them."

"Alice, do you have a granddaughter who lives here?"

Looking toward the picture on the table near the window, then back at Ashley, Alice replied, "I did, dear. My lovely granddaughter Grace lived with me until she…"

Alice raised her delicate fingers to her mouth to hide her sad expression. "Until she went to be with her parents. My dear sweet family has all gone to be with the Lord."

With both hands, Ashley raised the blanket to cover her mouth in an attempt to fight back the sadness once again building inside her.

Seeing Ashley getting upset again, Alice said, "Oh dear, it's been over ten years. God is good to me. Let's talk about you."

*You can do this*, Ashley thought. *Just tell her the positive stuff.* Ashley was preparing herself mentally for the onslaught of negative thoughts that might appear if she talked about her own life. Alice was so generous and kind, she had no choice but to share something with her.

"I have had a new job for a few months, and I'm up for a promotion. I hope I get it." Ashley said. "I've been running every night. I heard it's good for the mind as well as the body."

"I'm so happy to hear you speak of these things. Ashley, I'm very glad that you have been accepting my baskets of treats."

Ashley interrupted her, "About that Alice, I'm indebted to you…"

"Now stop right there, dear, let me explain something to you. I have been living alone for many years. I thank God for all that I have, and I trust him in all things. I believe you are here by His design, not your own. It has blessed me tremendously to fix you those baskets, and it is a joy to my heart to have you here right now."

Ashley could feel pressure rising in her heart, warming her.

Alice continued, "I have watched you sneak into that house all winter. I have prayed for you and your safety. God laid it on my heart to prepare a room for you. I had no idea when or how it would happen, but clearly, He had a plan. I want you to stay here with me until you get on your feet again, and I mean when you get enough money saved up to have your own place and a car. Until then, I'm going to take much pleasure in your company."

Alice paused and remained silent while Ashley absorbed all that she had just said.

Holding the blanket to her face again, tears fell from Ashley's eyes. Her heart was swelling with emotion so much that it propelled Ashley off the couch and over to Alice, leaving her blanket to fall on the floor. Ashley gave Alice a gentle but deep hug. Alice wrapped her arms around Ashley and assured her everything would be okay. They talked for a bit until they both grew sleepy.

Lying in an unfamiliar bed, in unfamiliar pajamas, Ashley felt strangely at home. As she walked through the events of the night in her mind, she thought about Alice. *If Alice had not been there, if she had not cared, if she had not trusted her God…*

Within seconds, Ashley was asleep. Alice saw her sleeping, turned off the hall light, and went to bed. "Thank you, Lord, for protecting Ashley from the fire. My cup runneth over."

# Emerging

Living with Alice had stirred a torrent of emotions in Ashley. One minute, she enjoyed the nurturing kindness, and the next, she wanted to run away and never come back. Her head was filling with unfamiliar thoughts and feelings of love and tenderness, but these things waged war against her self-determined need to keep her heart hostage and heavily guarded.

When Alice asked her to do some yard work, Ashley felt indebted and felt she had no choice but to comply. *Yard work! I hate yard work,* she thought. With bitterness building inside her and a fake smile on her face, Ashley went to the shed for the rake and a barrel. Walking along the herringbone brick walkway, she glimpsed its beautiful pattern and then made the connection to her own masonry work; the tower guarding her heart, the one built tall and thick so no one could reach what hurt the most to touch.

*Why do we fight what's right and good? Walls, walkways, what does it all matter?* These thoughts ran through Ashley's mind as she labored with the rake in Alice's front yard. While cleaning up the leaves, sticks, and branches from the harsh winter, her mind was full. With each pass of the rake, Ashley grew angry hearing the tines rip into the soil and tear at the folded blades of grass. Her teeth clenched together as pressure built in her cheeks. She tried to hold back the pain, even so, grunts escaped her as she slammed the metal rake harder and quicker with each stroke until she burst into a fit of frustration. Throwing the rake down, she let out an angry yell, "I hate this! I hate feeling this way."

Ashley wasn't used to having an array of emotions. She had barricaded herself from any kind of feelings for many years. Determined to fight back against the anger, she picked up the rake and finished the entire front yard. As she approached the edge near the road, she saw the bulldozers tearing down the house across the street.

Since living with Alice, Ashley learned that the house she had been living in across the street throughout the winter was not abandoned. Dr. Edward Brown had left it to Alice to watch while he went to Nevada to care for his only sister, who was undergoing cancer treatments. Dr. Brown lost his wife years ago to cancer, so it was important to him to be there for his sister in her time of need, as she was unmarried and had no children of her own. The fact that Dr. Brown's house had electricity and hot water finally made sense to Ashley after Alice explained the situation.

Seeing the demolition of the house had an even greater impact on Ashley's emotions now that she understood how much more was lost in the fire. Dr. Brown had four grown children. That house held all of their childhood memories, all of their photos, and everything else they'd saved over the years. Now everything was lost. *Everything's gone! They have nothing left. I have nothing left.* Once again, emotions took over. This time, tears streamed down her face.

The rumble of the mail truck had Ashley wiping her tears away as she grabbed the handle of the yard waste barrel.

"Good morning," he said as the truck rolled up to Alice's mailbox.

"Hi," she replied.

"Getting ready for the yard to become a masterpiece, I see," the mailman said.

With a puzzled look on her face, Ashley lifted her shoulders and hands in the I-don't-know-what-you-mean manner.

"You mean you've never seen this yard in the springtime when the flowers are in full bloom?" he asked.

"No, I just moved in."

"Well, you just wait and see. This is the most spectacular yard in the neighborhood, with so much beauty soon to be emerging."

With a charming smile, he said, "Have a good day," and then drove away.

Ashley looked back over the property and wondered what he was talking about. All she could see was yellowish-green grass now laced with brown dirt lifted from heavy raking. She dragged the barrel to the back of the garage and put the rake away in the shed.

Kicking off her shoes on the back steps and smacking her jeans, she gave herself a quick brush down before entering the house through the kitchen door. Alice had an ice-cold pitcher of lemonade sitting on the counter with a tall glass filled with ice next to it and a plate of oatmeal raisin cookies there as well. Alice loved to bake and always had treats for Ashley, no matter what time of day it was.

The sun shone through white eyelet curtains embroidered with petite green leaves, brightening the pale yellow walls of the kitchen. Fresh cut daisies in a milk glass vase, plainly visible from the living room, were also displayed on the counter.

"All finished?" Alice inquired.

"Yes, I finished the front yard."

"Alice, why do you think people hold onto so much memorabilia if it can all be destroyed in a moment?"

"Oh dear, are you referring to Dr. Brown's house?"

"I just don't understand why he left it all there. I don't understand why his children left their things in that house. If those things were so important to be kept all these years, why leave them there where no one sees them?"

Ashley paced between the front window in the living room and the kitchen as she asked these questions. Each time she passed near the window, she could see the tractors in the distance moving the remains of the house into a large dumpster.

"They've lost everything. Everything they thought was special enough to keep. It's all gone." Ashley cried out.

Alice knew Ashley was dealing with deeper issues of the heart, ones that Ashley herself needed to work through. She also knew that these questions emerging from Ashley's broken heart were the beginning of the healing process. Ashley had been in denial for many years. This fire was the trigger for her to release everything bottled up inside her.

Taking the plate of cookies from the counter and placing them on the table, Alice motioned for Ashley to take a seat with her. Ashley retrieved her glass and plopped down in one of the chairs. She seemed mentally drained and in desperate need of encouragement.

"Ashley, dear, our most treasured things in life are not things at all. They are the love we carry in our hearts for people. The things lost in that fire were only symbols of the love Dr. Brown and his family share. They are a very close family, full of wonderful memories that they reminisce over regularly. Their stories remain alive as long as they keep sharing them, and it keeps their love alive, too. No one is ever truly gone as long as we carry them in our hearts."

*No one is ever truly gone as long as we carry them in our hearts.* Ashley replayed those words in her mind over and over. Rising from her chair, Ashley set her glass on the table and said, "Please excuse me, I need to take a shower before I dirty up your clean house," and she walked down the hall.

Alice walked over to the bay window, wrapped her arms across her chest, and embraced the memories she held with Ed. Before his sister grew sick with cancer, Alice and Ed spent most of their time together. It was comforting for them being widows and living without their families. They were sweet companions, went on trips together, enjoyed meals together, and most importantly, shared memories of their families with each other. Alice knew Dr. Brown's family very well, simply from the memories he shared over the years.

Alice knew what she needed to do to help Ashley, and she devised a plan for the evening. When Ashley returned to the kitchen, Alice asked her, "Would you like to join me for a movie tonight? I have one in mind, but I don't know how to find it."

Since Ashley didn't have work, she was interested in the movie night. "I'd love to watch a movie with you."

"I sure hope you can find it," Alice replied.

"I'll check the library first, and if they don't have it, I'll go to FYE," Ashley answered.

"Could you pick up a few things for me at the grocery store when you go out?" Alice asked.

"Sure thing, and I can put gas in your car too."

"That would be lovely. I have an appointment tomorrow afternoon, and it would be nice not to worry about that."

Alice prayed as soon as Ashley left.

*Lord, please work through me to show Ashley the beauty of keeping loved ones alive in our hearts. She is on the verge of something, I feel it. Might it be Lord?*

It had been years since Alice had an evening like this. She pulled out the chocolate fountain maker, a platter for the fruit and long-handled mini forks. Excitement built in Alice as she prepared for the movie night with Ashley. Memories flooded her mind of these wonderful nights with Grace, her granddaughter. They didn't happen often, but when they did have chocolate-covered movie nights, as they called them, it was very special.

Alice recalled one particular time with Grace after her parents were killed in a car accident. Grace had kept to herself and had gone quite dark for some time. That's when Alice came up with a chocolate-covered movie night. She imagined it was the wonder of seeing the chocolate flowing over the tiers of the fountain, not a sight you get to see too often. Or maybe it was the intrigue of chocolate-covered potato chips that broke the walls down for Grace. Whatever it was, Alice remembered the laughter and smiles, and she remembered the movie giving Grace a different perspective. Grace saw how families cope with the loss of loved ones, and she welcomed the new way of remembering good memories instead of replaying the accident.

"I found everything, Alice: the movie, the fruit, the pretzels, marshmallows, chocolate, even the spicy chips you asked for. I am so curious now what all of this is for," Ashley said as she carried the groceries into the kitchen. Then she saw the chocolate fountain machine, and with a telling smile said, "No way!"

Alice chuckled at Ashley's realization of what was to become chocolate-covered everything. Ashley was already celebrating just thinking about it. Both ladies giggled at the thought of such an indulgence.

Alice got busy right away with getting the fruit prepared and onto the platter.

"Ashley, can you figure out how to get the movie to work in that movie player under the television?"

Smiling at Alice's use of words, Ashley said, "No problem, Alice. I'll get the DVD player working."

Once everything was ready, including the melted chocolate flowing over the rim of the fountain, Alice announced that it was now time to get into their most comfortable pajamas.

"This early, Alice? Before dinner?"

"Yes, dear, tonight, this is dinner," Alice said while pointing at the decadent spread of fruit and snacks on the counter.

Ashley couldn't wipe the smile off her face as she went to her room to get into her pink plaid pjs. Returning to the kitchen, she let out the biggest laugh when she saw Alice in pale green fleece pajamas with pigs on them.

"Oh, Alice! I had no idea you had pajamas like that. Pigs?"

"It's quite appropriate for our extravagant chocolate-covered movie night, don't you think?"

Alice said with a smirk, then let out a gentle laugh. *Pig out, I get it,* Ashley thought, but didn't say it.

"Yes, they look comfortable and fun, and this looks like we are going to have a blast," Ashley replied.

Each fixed a collection of chocolate-covered goodies and then settled down for the movie in the living room. In this moment, Ashley had forgotten all about her hurting heart. She was savoring the sweetness and contemplating the complex flavors exploding on her tongue.

"Alice, I had no idea spicy nacho flavored chips would taste so good covered in chocolate." *Did I just hear that right?* She immediately thought. Then she burst out laughing. She laughed so hard she had to cover her mouth so nothing would escape it. Grabbing her drink, she washed everything down and gathered her composure.

Soon, Ashley would be seeing the power of cherishing good memories and letting them heal the brokenness in life instead of guarding the heart and letting it wither away from starvation and neglect. The heartwarming movie beautifully represented a family reminiscent of good times filled with laughter, love, and tenderness. Only near the end does one realize that the people in the movie are not alive but only memories. The lady reliving these memories was living proof that keeping the good things alive in her heart and mind was essential to keeping herself alive.

Ashley felt rumbling in her own heart, as if the walls were beginning to crumble. *How can this be happening? I don't want this. I don't want to let the walls down.* It seemed the heart was more powerful than Ashley's mind thought possible. It had been nurtured and soon began to draw from the joy Ashley allowed into her thoughts. It wasn't Ashley's will that made the walls crumble, it was her heart expanding beyond the stronghold it had formed.

Feeling overwhelmed, she excused herself, "Alice, I need to be alone. I'm sorry. I'll help clean up in the morning," and she immediately went to her bedroom.

Closing the door, she dropped to the bed, stuck her face in the pillow and let out a muffled scream. The rumbling she was feeling inside terrified her. The thoughts swirling in her mind were so intense she could only cry as she clenched the pillow, exhausting herself.

As she drifted off to sleep, she imagined a man taking the bricks from the crumbled pile and laying them in a beautiful herringbone pattern on the walkway. She watched in awe as he made something beautiful and inviting out of something that had been destroyed. She saw the walkway and realized that her heart needed to welcome visitors, not keep them out.

# Beauty Prevails

Alice had a feeling something was wrong, so instead of driving to the appointment she had for 9 AM, she drove herself to the emergency room. She never got out of the car, though. A concerned citizen reported her odd posture in the car to the security guard who was patrolling the lot. He called into the ER, and they came out with a stretcher to get her.

"Alice, can you hear me?" the nurses kept repeating as they rushed her into the hospital from the parking lot.

She felt the jostling of her body and heard someone calling her name, but she couldn't respond. She was somewhere else. There was a black and white scene playing out in Alice's mind of a woman rocking a small child in her lap. The soothing, gentle sounds of the woman singing comforted the child, who was crying and clinging to the woman. The woman rubbed her warm hands over the child's back. Both found solace in each other in their time of grief, one lost a husband, the other a father.

"Alice, can you hear me?" asked a nurse. In that moment, the scene changed in Alice's mind.

There were lots of sirens and flashing lights, people screaming and crying, and bodies lying on the ground in pools of blood. A police officer was covering the bodies. Seeing her daughter like that was an unbearable pain for Alice to endure.

"She's coding," announced another nurse.

The image now before Alice was of a casket and her granddaughter, Grace, lying there. Death was sweeping through Alice's mind and body, even as the nurses shocked her heart and put her on oxygen to keep her alive.

"We got her back. Let's get her stabilized," stated a nurse.

Elsewhere, Ashley returned home after work, surprised to see a pickup truck parked in front of the garage with no one sitting in it. Looking around, she proceeded cautiously into the house.

Startled to find someone sitting in the living room, Ashley exclaimed, "Oh! I didn't expect to find someone in here. You must have a key."

Rising to shake her hand and introduce himself, he walked toward Ashley as she shut the door.

"I'm David Brown, and yes, I have a key. You must be Ashley."

His warm hand grasped hers in a gentle but hearty handshake, sending a chill up her arm.

"Yes, I am. Are you Dr. Brown from across the street?"

Smiling, he replied, "No, I am his son, the youngest of four."

"Why are you here? And where is Alice? She's usually making dinner around now."

"Ashley, please come sit down, I need to tell you something," David told Ashley about Alice, and immediately they went to the hospital.

In David's truck, Ashley felt like her whole world had just turned black again. She remained silent as he drove.

"When my dad went to Nevada to help my aunt, he asked me to be available should Alice need anything. After the hospital called him today, he called me and told me about you."

"Dr. Brown knows about me?" Ashley asked.

"Of course he does. He and Alice are very close. He told me you were living with her, so I came right over."

Ashley suddenly felt awkward. Shrinking into her sweatshirt, she looked out the window and wondered how much David knew about her. She also wondered how much Dr. Brown knew.

Looking at Ashley, David sensed her discomfort and explained something to her.

"Ashley, my dad was glad you found refuge in his house."

Pulling her hood over her head and her face, she curled up into a ball, tucking her knees up under her chin. Shame and humiliation caused her to retreat in time in her thoughts.

"You don't know anything about my dad, do you?" David asked. Ashley did not reply.

"My dad was abandoned as a child. He knows the hard life. He was taken in by a family who showed him unconditional love and acceptance. They raised him and encouraged him to believe he could achieve whatever he set his heart and mind on. Because of their love and provisions for him, he determined himself to become a doctor and an advocate for young people in similar situations. He founded an organization to protect, provide for, and promote those individuals who, like him, have a real desire to succeed and determination to do so, even in the face of adversity."

Ashley sat up, pushed her hood back, and looked over at David. Trying to take in all of this information on top of the news about Alice, she couldn't speak; she just looked at him. David understood she needed time to absorb all that was going on. He didn't say anything else. They drove to the hospital in silence the rest of the way. As they pulled into the emergency room parking lot, Ashley asked, "Have you been to see her yet?"

"No, I went to get you first. I knew you would have no way of knowing where she was."

"Thank you," she replied.

Sitting in the hospital room alone with Alice, Ashley replayed every conversation she ever had with her. From the first knock at the door in the frigid winter at Dr. Brown's house, to the fire, to the chocolate-covered movie night, Ashley remembered it all. Without Alice awake to comfort her, Ashley found comfort in her words from the last few months. She remembered how calm Alice was during the fire and how she told her it was all part of God's plan.

Over the years, David had seen Alice on occasion but generally gave his father privacy concerning his personal life. David lived two hours away in the city and had no other reason to travel to the suburbs, unless his father was in town.

Light filtered into the room from the hallway as David poked his head in to ask Ashley to come out so they could talk. They walked to a private waiting room where David explained all that was going on with Alice. He told Ashley the devastating news that Alice suffered a major heart attack and might not make it through the night. David caught Ashley when she collapsed from the shock of the news. He held her as she cried. Realizing the time was running out for Alice, David forced the situation to move on. He pulled away from Ashley and reached into his pocket, retrieving car keys and an envelope.

"Ashley, I have to leave now. You need to spend time with Alice to say goodbye. When you are ready, you also need to read this letter. It is from her. These are her car keys, so you can drive yourself home."

"Please don't leave," Ashley pleaded.

"I must go. You have to do this on your own. I will be in touch." With that said, he lowered his head and walked out of the room. Ashley stood there looking at the letter and keys in her hand. Then she remembered Alice and ran down the hall to her room.

Seeing her chest rising and falling to the sound of the ventilator and seeing her heart rhythm on the monitor comforted Ashley. She took a seat next to the bed, stared at Alice for a while, and then opened the letter.

*If you are reading this letter, it means I am incapacitated and Dr. Brown or his son has my personal items and this letter. As I write this, I do not know who you are. However, as you read it, please know that I do know who you are, and you are very special to me. You see, there were very specific guidelines to follow that preceded the designation of this letter, which means if you are reading it, I trust you. It means I have gotten to know you, and I've spoken to Dr. Brown about you. It also means that I have prayed for you, and God has appointed you to be the one to receive this letter.*

*I'm dying. It won't be long now before I go. I am leaving some of my possessions with you to care for and use under strict rules. As long as you abide by the rules, you may use my car, my house, and have access to some of my money.*

*Dr. Brown will be in touch with you to discuss the details, as they fall under his organization's mission, and he has the power of attorney over my assets.*

*Please continue living as you have been. I have left things for you to discover. I have no other family, so all that is left is for you. I'm quite certain that as you discover my journals and read them, you will gain a fuller, deeper understanding of the purpose in all of this. Your future rests on your determination to persevere. You are now on your own and have been given the greatest opportunity of your life. Thank you for coming into my life. You are a part of His plan, and I have prayed for your future success.*

*May He always be your guide,*
*Alice*

With tears streaming down her face, Ashley placed the letter down and climbed onto the bed and lay down next to Alice. She had not felt this close to anyone in years. As unnatural as it was for Ashley to give in to her heart's need for affection, she could not deny this need to love Alice, even if it was in her last moments. Ashley held onto her tightly and wept as if she could somehow let Alice know how much she cared. Maybe Alice could feel it.

"Alice, please don't leave me. You're the only one I have. You mean the world to me… Alice… (sobbing)… NO… Alice…please….no…"

Ashley cried every tear she had, then lifted her face to whisper in Alice's ear, "I love you, Alice." Then she pressed her face to Alice's, closed her eyes, and just let the love flow between them. Soon, Ashley fell asleep next to Alice.

BEEEEEEP!! BEEEEEP!!! BEEP! BEEP! BEEP!!! Alarms and beepers sounded, causing Ashley to jump off the bed. Seeing the flatline on the heart monitor caused Ashley to scream "NO" as nurses came running in. Ashley stepped back and trembled as the doctors attempted to resuscitate Alice, only to ultimately pronounce her deceased.

Turning all of the machines off and disconnecting them from Alice, the nurses tidied up Alice's bedding and let Ashley have a few minutes alone. Ashley's heart was in her throat. She held Alice's hand, lifted it to her mouth, and kissed it. She could not say goodbye. She stood there numb and void of any further thoughts or feelings. Everything had turned black.

After riding around in the car for hours, numb from the pain of losing Alice, thoughts began racing through Ashley's mind. There was so much she didn't understand, so many unanswered questions, and now this peculiar situation unfolding with her new opportunity, as Alice called it. Somehow, without her intent, Ashley found herself pulling into the driveway at the house. Stunned at what she saw, Ashley stopped the car, got out, and looked around in pure amazement.

Flowers were in full bloom everywhere. There were waves of purple across the lush green grass, explosions of pink and white tree blossoms along the skyline, blue and purple climbing clematis around the lamp post and mailbox, fragrant lilac bushes flanking both sides of the property, hydrangeas and tulips accented the shrubs in front of the house, and purple phlox lined the driveway and walkways creating the masterpiece the mailman told her about a few weeks ago. All of this beauty invaded Ashley's senses. On this day, when her world had turned black, these flowers decided to reveal themselves to her. The euphoria it created made it impossible for Ashley to resist. She was feeling a sense of joy that fought against her broken heart and distraught mind.

When she thought she would return to Alice's house to mourn and wallow in the darkness of her grief, this breathtaking display of beauty overtook her and shed the light and love of Alice's hard work. A peaceful feeling swept over her as she walked through the yard, taking in all the colorful sights and smells.

Ashley rocked on the porch swing, allowing the abundance of this beauty to wash over the darkness encompassing her,6 thus creating a new picture, a new reality, a new perspective of life and death, and love. Then she thought, *in life as in death, beauty prevails*.

# Always Remember

*You're never gonna make it. Look at yourself sitting here in someone else's house all alone. You have nothing. You have no one. You're a failure.*

"It's not true!" Ashley yelled in response to her thoughts.

Rising from the chair and shaking off the negative thoughts, she knew she needed to get out of the house. *I need to run,* she thought. Immediately, Ashley changed her clothes and laced up her sneakers. Within minutes, she was down the road for an evening run through the back roads. These runs were like a familiar friend to her. Many times, when life became exceedingly emotional, whether good or bad, she achieved a balance by running.

Much had happened since Alice passed: the funeral, meeting Dr. Brown for the first time, living in Alice's house without Alice. Yet, the thing that had Ashley's mind racing was all that Dr. Brown had told her about what Alice had left her. As if meeting him after the fire wasn't enough emotional drama, Ashley had a three-hour discussion with him and his son, David. They went over every detail of Alice's estate. There were so many rules, so many high expectations she needed to live up to, and so many emotions she was experiencing because of this generous offer from not only Alice, but also from Dr. Brown's foundation. Ashley became overwhelmed. *I'm not ready for this. I'm not strong enough. I've only just started getting used to working and living with Alice and spending time with someone who cares about me. This is too much. I can't do it.*

Ashley let all of these thoughts work their way out of her. For once, she didn't stop them. She didn't fight against them. She wanted to acknowledge them all. Her pace picked up the more negative her thoughts became. She pressed in harder and faster into her run. Her breathing grew deeper as sweat ran down the sides of her face and her back. After quite some time, she began to slow down. Her thoughts fell in sync with her pace. When she slipped into the zone and rhythm of a jog, she felt a sense of relief. Then, for a few miles, Ashley had no thoughts at all.

That's when her positive self-talk returned. In an audible cheer, she exclaimed, "I can do this! I can do this for Alice. I can do this for Dr. Brown. I can do this for me!"

She smiled as she turned the last corner onto the homestretch. *I will bring Alice honor, that's what I'll do, and Dr. Brown too. I will do my very best.*

Once she reached the yard, Ashley took a long look at the house and yard, inhaled a deep breath, and then entered the house to rest a bit.

Discovering Alice's journals had been enlightening for Ashley. She found some mixed in with gardening books on the corner shelf in the office. There were quite a few, but they were separated and spread out along several shelves. Finding the oldest, most worn journal, Ashley sat down to begin discovering what exactly Alice wanted her to know.

*Saturday, October 8, 1948*

*Today, Henry brought home a sack of bulbs to be planted in our yard. He explained that when the tulips bloom each year, we will have an occasion to remember our first year in the new house. Such a tender heart, my Henry. He told me about Walter and Beatrice, the kind people who gave him the bulbs from their garden. They gave him the idea to start the gardening tradition from year one, since we were newlyweds. I am blessed to have married such a thoughtful man.*

Under the journal entry was an old picture of Alice's house taped to the page. The only flowers in the yard were two bunches of pink tulips, one on each side of the stairs. Ashley smiled, realizing the stories these journals must hold since the yard is full now. She read a few more pages. Her heart swelled as she realized how loving Alice and Henry were. There were even a few pictures of them together in the yard. Ashley closed the journal and held it to her chest, closed her eyes, and imagined hugging Alice. *Oh, how I missed her,* Ashley thought.

Then her thoughts jumped to the dream she had about meeting a man of her own. She pondered the possibilities. *Who would want me? I'm nowhere near as nice as Alice, and I have never met anyone as respectful and loving as Henry; besides, I have nothing to offer. Who am I anyway?* With these thoughts came a barrage of self-deprecating attacks. There was no stopping her mind today; the mood swings were going berserk. She decided to listen to some music as she made dinner for herself. Music always offered an escape. She was coming apart at the seams. She was sitting in the living room again, remembering the movie night with Alice, yet now feeling so alone. There was no one to comfort her.

She had been fighting this battle all day. Accepting defeat, she resolved to simply go to bed early. Walking down the hall, instead of going to her room, she went to Alice's. Standing in the doorway, she reached in and turned on the light, and then saw another journal on the nightstand. Ashley stood for a few minutes trying to decide if she wanted to learn anything else today. Her heart was aching, but her mind was exhausted. Thinking she might find comfort in this room, she decided to lie down on Alice's bed. She dropped face down into the pillow for a few minutes until she needed air. Turning her head, she put both arms around the pillow, then just hugged it. Tears fell from her eyes as she remembered lying in the hospital bed with Alice the night she died.

After dozing off for a few minutes, Ashley's eyes landed on the journal. Sitting up, she grabbed it and opened it to the last page written and noticed both sides of the open book had the same date: one side started off with *Dear Lord* and the other *Dearest Ashley*. Gasping at the sight of her name in Alice's journal, Ashley closed the book, unsure if she could handle any more emotional input.

*She wrote to me in her journal? Me? Why me?* After a few minutes, she reopened the journal and read the part to God first. The words were very personal and heartfelt. It was a prayer to God for the needs of people, but she was also giving him thanks for answered prayer. *This sounds like she was talking to her mother or father,* Ashley thought. The words to God were intimate and written without fear of judgment, as if they had a close personal relationship. Ashley had never heard someone talk that way before. It was strange but comforting. It gave her a peaceful feeling to read Alice's private words to God. Then she took a deep breath and began reading the other page.

*Dearest Ashley,*

*Today I woke up feeling a terrible pain in my chest with an uncomfortable heaviness. I didn't want you to worry about me, so I didn't tell you at breakfast. I did my best to smile and enjoyed your laughter over the odd shape of the pancakes and the spilled orange juice. I am so blessed to have you here. You add so much joy to my life. I'm still smiling just thinking about your happiness this morning.*

*I have an appointment to see the doctor, but I'm going to the hospital instead. I just don't feel right. I wanted to write this to you in case, well, if this is it. Ashley, dear, I will be thinking of your smile and hearing your laughter as I head out. You are with me. I cherish your friendship, and I love you dearly.*

*Always remember.*

Streams of tears rolled down Ashley's face as she considered Alice's last words. *What does she mean by always remember? Always remember what?* Then it flashed through her mind – the terrible feelings she had when Dr. Brown's house burned down. Ashley recalled trying to understand how Dr. Brown's family could deal with losing everything in the fire. She remembered Alice telling her, "No one is ever truly gone as long as we carry them in our hearts." *Alice knew I would feel this way. She knew I would feel like I lost everything all over again. She's telling me to always remember her and to tell her stories. That's it! She's telling me to read her journals and tell her stories, and that will keep her with me. She already explained that to me. That is why she has these journals. She has kept Henry alive in her heart all these years because she kept the memories alive. She told the stories. Yes! She and Dr. Brown shared stories of their families. She told me stories about her granddaughter, Grace. She was keeping Grace alive in her heart. Oh, I get it, Alice!*

With this new revelation, Ashley's heart leapt with joy. She was smiling. She knew how much she loved Alice, but she was just now realizing how important she was to Alice. They really were together in spirit; their hearts were joined. The love was real. Ashley hadn't lost everything. In fact, at this moment, she realized the depth of what she had received. It was more than Alice's property or an opportunity to succeed. It was worth more than all of Alice's assets combined. Ashley had been given the gift of love, and she had only just begun receiving it.

Ashley once again recalled Alice's words, *Love does not die with death, always remember.*

# Beautiful Mess

"Ashley, hold up."

"Hi Brian, what's up? Need me to take something to the print shop? That's where I'm heading."

"No, I have been trying to catch up with you for days. You're in and out so quickly it's nearly impossible."

"Yes, my new position keeps me very busy. What did you need me for?"

Running a few steps in front of her and stopping so she would stop walking, Brian looked her in the eyes and boldly asked her out to dinner. With no time to waste, he was specific and asked for dinner that night or the next.

"That's a great idea. Can I get back to you once I'm back in the office?"

"Sure, you have my number. Thanks, Ashley. Talk to you later."

*Whew, I played that off cool. Did Brian Weston just ask me to dinner? How is this even possible? He's the hottest guy in the office.* Ashley took a deep breath and refocused on what she needed to do at work. There was no time to daydream with her new schedule.

One foot in the door back in her office, and the phone was already ringing. "Yes, this is Ashley. Okay, Mr. Benson, 6 pm Thursday at the Omni. Got it. Thank you, sir." Penciling in her calendar, the phone rang again. "Yes, I realize your time constraints. I will make sure it gets delivered to you by 7 pm tonight, even if I have to bring it myself. I will, sir. Yes. Thank you." Without placing the phone in the cradle, Ashley pressed the extension to the print shop.

"Josh, this is Ashley. I need the Vandal order completed ASAP. It needs to be a top priority and delivered before 6:30 tonight. I know you're backed up, just make it happen." As she hung up the phone, she noticed she had eighteen email notifications blinking on her computer.

Immersing herself in her work, she remained busy until she got the call from Josh at 6:15. "Ashley, the Vandal order is ready, but the courier service said it would be an hour before they could pick up."

"Can you deliver it, Josh?"

"Sorry, I took the metro in today."

"Okay, bring the order to the parking garage. My car is on level D, city side. Be there in five minutes."

Ashley made it to the Vandal headquarters by 6:45 pm and was completely relieved once she handed over the documents to the secretary; then she headed home. After her evening run and a shower, she settled down with some leftovers for dinner and opened her laptop to finish what she was working on earlier back at the office so as not to leave projects open over the weekend.

Like most homeowners in suburbia, Saturdays were set aside for yard work. After reading Alice's gardening journals over the last several weeks, Ashley felt a strong connection to every plant, rock, flower, and tree in the yard. She did all of the work herself, including mowing, edging, pruning, fertilizing, and watering. *I hope Alice is proud of my work*, Ashley thought as she stood along the edge of the street, looking over the expanse of landscape. The rumbling of the mail truck caused her to step away from the road.

"Very impressive," he said as he drove up, stopping midway between the driveway and the mailbox, handing Ashley a stack of mail.

"What is?" she asked.

"All of the work you've been doing. The yard looks as perfect as it always has."

"Alice left detailed instructions. I would have it no other way. Did she ever tell you about the weeping cherry tree?" Ashley asked.

"No, she told me a few things over the years, mostly about how much she loved working in the yard. I just figured she loved gardening."

"Did she ever tell you about Henry or Grace?"

"No. Like I said, she told me about the blue delphiniums along the wall here. She told me how they reminded her of summer nights at the drive-up soda fountain. She told me about the sunflowers over there and how she loved to watch the birds eat the seeds in the fall. Who are Henry and Grace?"

"Do you have time to have some lemonade? I'd love to tell you." Ashley asked with a bright smile on her face.

"Well, I don't have time, but I sure would love some lemonade. Let me pull the truck over."

Ashley waited and then walked with him toward the house. "You know, I don't even know your name," she said with a slight flush on her cheeks. Then giggled and covered her mouth.

"Greg. Funny how I never have to ask people their names, so I forget to tell them mine."

Stopping at the steps of the porch, Ashley turned, extended her hand, and said, "Nice to meet you, Greg. Have a seat, and I'll bring out the lemonade."

She walked in the house, made it around the corner, and then let out a full-body shiver. Everything about Greg was making her feel tingly. *This is not happening. The mailman named Greg is not really sitting on my porch waiting for a glass of lemonade right now. Breathe, Ashley, breathe.*

Ashley brought the lemonade in Alice's old-fashioned glass pitcher with two tall ice-filled glasses on a matching tray out to the little table on the front porch. She handed one glass to Greg and took one for herself. She sat down and began right away, telling him who Henry and Grace were. She told Greg the highlights of the sentimentality of the garden, and she told him about the weeping cherry tree, how it was planted in memory of Grace.

After 20 minutes, Greg stood and explained that he had to get back to work. "I'd love to hear more stories about Alice someday," he said as he handed her the empty glass, "but I must get back to work."

"I'd love to tell you," Ashley said with an endearing smile.

"Maybe you can come back after work?" Ashley suggested before considering that Greg might be married. Upon realizing what she had just asked, she turned beet-red and began apologizing for being inconsiderate.

Greg's smile revealed his perfectly straight teeth and dimples. "No need to be embarrassed. I'm not married. I'd love to come back. I've enjoyed this talk immensely."

Ashley said goodbye and let Greg walk back to the mail truck alone. She stood there holding their empty glasses as he drove away. Then she put the glasses on the tray, sat on the swing, and daydreamed.

Running household errands on Saturday afternoon was a chore Ashley didn't enjoy. *Who really likes buying toilet paper and cleaning supplies at a store crowded with screaming children wanting something their mother said they couldn't have?* she thought. Yet, this is the life she now lives as someone managing a home.

To make it less of a burden, Ashley rewarded herself with a fruit smoothie on the drive home. It was a stress relief just walking in the door of the shoppe as good music played and people relaxed in cozy chairs, chatting with their friends. Happy faces filled this environment. Taking a cleansing breath as she pulled the door open and walked in, Ashley found herself face-to-face with David Brown. "Wow, what a surprise to see you here, David."

"Ashley!" he said with a shrill of delight and immediately gathered her into a tight hug. Releasing her, but leaving his hand on her shoulders, David looked into her eyes with deep compassion and asked, "How are you doing?"

He hadn't seen her since the meeting with his father after the funeral. He had sent a few emails, but had no obvious reason to be back in town. "I'm doing great, David, really great," She said with a smile.

"That's wonderful."

"Have you ordered yet?" she asked and pointed towards the fruit display.

"I was going to when I saw you walking in. Let's go get our drinks before we talk anymore. I need a power punch smoothie right now," he said with a chuckle.

Ashley ordered a tropical delight and explained that she would love to be on the beach in Hawaii. "What brings you to town, David?"

Smiling and hesitating to reveal his news, David took another slow sip of his smoothie and let his eyes linger on Ashley's overall beauty. He seemed at peace and very content in the moment.

"I had a meeting with a contractor who is going to be rebuilding my dad's house." David stopped there to let Ashley absorb the news.

"Wow, you're gonna rebuild the house. Are you gonna sell it when it's done?"

"Actually, I've decided to live there."

Ashley choked on her drink and covered her mouth to clear her throat when she heard him say he was going to live across the street. "Sorry, it went down the wrong pipe."

Smiling again, David continued, "Yes, you'll be seeing a lot of me over the summer. I've hired a reputable team and have offered them a good price to get it completed before winter. I plan on moving in before Thanksgiving."

Ashley's mind suddenly remembered Greg and her invitation to him to return after work. Checking her phone for the time and gesturing at the surprise, she stated, "That's wonderful news. I am sorry to have to end this conversation abruptly, but I have company coming over soon. I have to get back to the house."

Rising to hug him goodbye, she finished by saying she looked forward to seeing him around, and he was welcome to come over when in the neighborhood.

Driving home, Ashley thought, *David, across the street. Wow.* She had the strangest feelings swirling over this news, but she couldn't figure them out. Dismissing the thought altogether, she focused on getting back before Greg returned.

Greg arrived at Ashley's house around 7 pm Saturday. He had showered and changed into loose-fitting khaki shorts, a button-down baby blue shirt, and flip-flops. He arrived with a small bunch of Marguerite daisies simply tied with a piece of twine. "For you," he said as he handed them to her.

"You were so thoughtful this afternoon to offer me lemonade. I wanted to show you my appreciation."

Ashley thanked Greg and found a short vase to put the flowers in. She set them on the coffee table and invited Greg to have a seat. There was already a pitcher of sweet tea on a serving tray with homemade cookies in the living room.

As they talked about Alice's stories, Greg seemed genuinely interested. At one point before dark, he asked Ashley to walk around the yard so he could visualize the stories she had told him. They were taken up in emotions at the beauty of Alice's masterpiece.

As darkness settled in, Ashley lit some candles that were scattered around the porch. When she returned to sit down, she found Greg sitting on the swing, patting the seat next to him for her to come join him. She did, and he rocked them. Ashley found herself wrapped in the arms of Greg with her head resting on his shoulder.

"This is nice," he said as he gently pushed the swing back and forth with his feet. She had pulled her knees up and was snuggled up under his arm in a warm embrace.

"It is," was barely heard as Ashley dozed off.

Greg's phone vibrated in his pocket and woke Ashley up. She jumped to a sitting position. In this moment, they both agreed to call it a night and said goodbye without any further physical contact.

"Thanks for a lovely evening, Ashley. This has been a wonderful day all around."

"Thanks, Greg, for taking the time to listen. It means more than you know. Have a nice rest of your weekend."

From the open doorway, she waited for Greg to drive away and then blew out all the candles and went straight to her bedroom.

After a month of reading Alice's journals, Ashley decided to start writing in one. She didn't write to God, and she didn't write to anyone in particular. In a way, she was just writing to herself. It was yet another one of those mind games she used to learn how to deal with life. Not having anyone close to work out her thoughts with, she usually took the task of writing to herself.

*My life has just bloomed with color, just like the yard! Greg, the mailman, is genuine, warm, and friendly, and very easy on the eyes. He is such a gentleman, too. I am so surprised he was interested in Alice's stories.*

Ashley daydreamed again for a few minutes, then resumed.

*Can't forget running into David Brown today either. Wow. I cannot believe he hugged me so tight. He acted like we had known each other for years. There was something very familiar about being near him. When we talked, something moved in me that I can't quite figure out. I am kind of excited that he's gonna be around more. Maybe then I'll be able to figure this out. He is so handsome!*

Just when she was about to shut the journal, the image of Brian popped into her head. *Oh no! I never got back to Brian this week. Brian Weston asked me out, and I totally blew him off. I cannot believe I did that. I played it off so cool when he asked me, he probably thinks I'm...*

Suddenly, her beautiful masterpiece was getting muddied. As she thought about the beautiful colors that were all crashing together, she began to draw a different image in her mind. *If David moves in across the street, and Greg is my mailman, and Brian wants to go out with me...*

With that thought, she stopped writing and closed the journal. She turned off the lamp, pulled up her blanket, and closed her eyes to sleep. *What would Alice do in the situation? She would make it all work out. This is one heck of a beautiful mess to be in, though.* Ashley smiled as she drifted off to sleep. Something was telling her everything would work out just perfectly.

# Dream Date

The day had finally arrived for the big date with Brian Weston. He accepted Ashley's apology when she called first thing Monday morning and explained that she would make it up to him. He offered to take her out once again for the upcoming Saturday night. She agreed.

Brian was taking Ashley to a restaurant in the city located on the rooftop of a high-rise hotel. It was the most exquisite and romantic place overlooking the city and the harbor. Their reservation was for 8 p.m.

Knowing she had nothing fancy enough to wear for this date, Ashley went to an upscale boutique and purchased a little black dress, high-heeled shoes, and some knock-off diamond earrings. The women at the boutique selected everything. They assured her that the diamond-trimmed open-back mini dress would accentuate her toned legs and her firm back. They also suggested she get her hair and nails done at the salon before her date, which she did Saturday afternoon.

Standing in front of the full-length mirror at home, Ashley felt like an actress all dolled up in costume for a play. Her hair was done up with wisps framing her face, and teardrop earrings sparkled along with the diamond studs on her dress. With her high-heeled shoes and red lipstick, she was ready for dinner and dancing at the top of the town. She felt like a princess.

Things were changing so fast in her life. She had a good job, a home, a car, money, and had enrolled in evening classes at a local college. Now that her life was coming together in a good way, she seemed to be attracting men. This date was her first, not counting the evening she spent with Greg, the mailman. This date was a real night on the town kind of date.

Her dream flashed in her mind, the dream where she had an encounter with Mr. Handsome on the train and then in her office building. She realized that she was going on a date with a real Mr. Handsome. Her dream was coming true. It was almost too good to be true. The doorbell chimed, and Ashley snapped out of her thoughts.

It was exactly 7 pm. Brian was prompt. Opening the door, she was greeted with an enormous bouquet of pink roses. Giggling with sheer delight, Ashley wrapped her arms around the bouquet and stepped back from the door to let Brian in.

"These roses are beautiful, but they're too much! I've never seen a bouquet this big in all my life."

Placing her nose in the center of the bunch and inhaling deeply, she allowed the fragrance to fill her. "They smell divine."

"I'm glad you like them," he said while walking towards the kitchen.

"Can I get a vase for you from somewhere?" Brian asked.

Ashley indicated where he could find one, and soon the roses were in freshwater. Wiping her hands on the kitchen towel, she smiled and scanned Brian's outfit. Starting with his square-tipped, leather Kenneth Cole shoes and working her way up to his well-fitted suit to his face, her eyes met with his approving smile.

They both spoke at the same time, causing them to laugh. They exchanged compliments and then Brian reached out his hand valiantly, "Shall we?"

"We shall," Ashley replied and let Brian walk her to the car.

Sitting in his BMW, Ashley once again felt like she was on the set of a movie and Brian was her gorgeous co-star. It all seemed too glamorous to be her reality. As Brian pulled out of the driveway, Ashley saw the cleared land across the street where Dr. Brown's house stood. It brought back memories of being in the basement, not having much of anything, not even emotions. She looked over at Brian and then down at her manicured nails and fancy outfit and knew she couldn't be happier than in this moment.

Driving into the city, Brian talked about himself for nearly the entire ride. He talked about all of his successes in life and never once asked about hers. Though she was impressed with Brian's achievements, she found herself bored with his extensive details. The conversation was completely one-sided. Ashley found herself losing interest quickly, which left her feeling unsure of what the rest of the night would be like. She found some relief by listening to music on the radio and looking out the window, occasionally looking at Brian and smiling.

As they approached the city, Brian changed the station to softer, more romantic music and stopped talking about himself. He looked over at Ashley, placed his hand on her knee, and stated how beautiful she looked. Not appreciating his hand touching her knee, she slipped her hand under his to break the contact, but then found herself holding his hand. He smiled at her again and gave her hand a little squeeze. Ashley blushed and smiled and turned her face to hide the oh-no-I-didn't-mean-to-do-that expression, even though she was still holding his hand.

"I hope you're ready to have a good time," Brian said as he released her hand to turn into the parking garage under the building.

Ashley smiled and quietly said, "I am."

Brian held Ashley's hand in the elevator up to the restaurant. She couldn't refuse now that she had just initiated the same contact in the car. They appeared to be a happy couple, even though it was their first date.

The reservation was for an intimate table for two, which meant the seats were adjacent, with both looking out over the harbor. The table was dressed with white linens, white candles, and the finest, delicate glassware. Their chairs were so close that their knees touched under the table. Brian had no place for his right arm, except across the back of her chair.

Ashley didn't refuse the wine when it was served. She also didn't let on that she had never had wine before. On this ever-growing, awkward date, she thought it would help her relax. She followed Brian's lead and drank as he did, figuring she would seem experienced. Feeling the warm sensation go through her as the wine went down only added more confusion to her thoughts. She was glad when the food came, not only to put something else in her stomach, but to wipe the bitter taste from her mouth. Ashley quickly decided she did not like wine.

When Brian was finished eating, he turned a little in his chair to look at Ashley. With his arm already around her back and his hand lingering near her shoulder, he couldn't resist running his fingers across her arm and up to her neck. He seemed to be entranced by her. He then leaned over to speak softly in her ear. Ashley silently gasped at what he said, lifted the napkin from her lap, placed it on the table, and excused herself to the ladies' room. As she walked through the restaurant, she noticed many eyes on her. She had one purpose, though, and that was to put space between her and Brian. Whoever was looking at her was irrelevant at the moment.

Once inside the ladies' room, Ashley set her clutch down, put both hands palm down on the counter, leaned over the sink, let out a deep sigh, and hung her head down to her chest. She remained a few seconds and then turned the water on to wash her hands. She would've loved to splash water on her face, but she couldn't smudge the makeup. Looking at herself in the mirror, she saw a woman who wasn't her.

This date was the most unnatural thing she had ever done. "I have two choices: make the best of it or let it get the best of me," she said under her breath.

Looking herself in the eyes, nodding her head in the affirmative as if in agreement with her thoughts, Ashley took out her lipstick, reapplied it, and said, "Make the best of it."

With the renewed attitude, she confidently walked back to the table. Brian stood when she arrived and swept her off to the dance floor before she could sit down. She gave a slight chuckle with a big smile and reassured him that she was indeed interested in dancing.

Another secret she kept to herself was that she had no idea how to dance. She did hear from the ladies in the boutique that all she had to do was relax and let the man lead. Brian was an excellent dancer. He commanded the floor as he seemed to carry Ashley across, beautifully twirling her and dipping her, and pulling her in for a few steps. She was exhilarated by his ability to move her body without effort. She was having a good time and once again felt like a princess.

They danced a few songs and then went back to the table for a drink. Drinking wine and dancing for over an hour. This time, when they went back out onto the dance floor, a slow song played, and Brian pulled her in tight. In a sweeping romantic dance move, he lifted and draped her arm around his neck and then dropped his around her waist, resting his hand on her lower back. That swift move left Ashley feeling uncomfortable once again. She would have preferred to dance more traditionally, not so close. She felt his legs up against hers, and his hand kept her pressed up against him. They moved as one, and she did not like it. When she felt his hand caress her bare back, that was it; she put her hand on his shoulder and pushed him away a little so she could once again excuse herself.

"I think the wine is getting to me. I'll be right back."

She walked off in the direction of the ladies' room, leaving Brian on the dance floor. Several minutes later, she returned to the table where Brian was having another glass of wine. "Are you okay?" he asked.

"Yes, I'm fine. I just needed to use the restroom. Too much wine," she said with a smile.

"Maybe it's time we call it a night," Brian suggested, waiting to see how Ashley would respond.

"I think you're right. I've had a lot of fun, but I'm feeling a bit tired," she said.

Smiling and gazing into her eyes, Brian tipped his head to the side, raised one eyebrow, and said, "I have the perfect remedy for that."

Then he stood and offered his hand to guide her out of the restaurant. At the elevator, Brian wrapped his arms around Ashley's shoulders in a bear hug. She didn't refuse this one because his embrace warmed her from the chill she was feeling in the elevator. She closed her eyes and just let his body heat warm her.

When the door opened and they walked down the hall, Ashley did not realize which floor they got off on. When Brian swiped a plastic card to gain entry into a room and led her in, that is when she figured out they were in a hotel room. To her surprise, she began to speak, but Brian suddenly kissed her, not allowing her to object to his decision about getting a room. Brian's hands were all over Ashley. He was suffocating her with his kiss until she finally maneuvered her hand up his chest and pushed with all of her might to break free from his embrace.

"What are you doing?" she yelled as she wiped her mouth of his saliva.

"What's wrong with you? I thought this was what you wanted," he shouted back in frustration. "You even said you would make it up to me when you apologized for blowing me off," Brian reminded her.

"This is not what I had in mind!" Ashley marched off to the bathroom and slammed the door. Once inside, she saw the tub filled with bubbles and a bottle of champagne set for two on the edge with candles everywhere. Looking around the bathroom in shock, Ashley realized that Brian had prearranged all of this. *He must've called ahead from the restaurant to have it timed perfectly,* she thought.

"He has taken this too far," she mumbled to herself.

Taking a deep breath and exhaling, Ashley knew she needed to get out of there. She phoned a cab and steeled herself for another gross attack by Brian. She told herself to make a beeline for the door and was ready to fight him off if need be. Righting her posture, she opened the door and headed for the door to leave the hotel room. She almost made it out when she felt his hand on her wrist. He stopped her midway through the door.

Ashley looked back at him and said, "Sorry, Brian, you had me figured wrong. I'm going home."

"I can't let you leave, just stay, we can just enjoy the luxury of the room. I'll let you sleep. You can trust me."

"No, Brian. Please let me go," Ashley said as she firmly tugged on her arm, freeing herself from his grip.

Reluctantly, he released her, and she marched straight towards the elevator. As she stepped into the elevator, she heard him yell out expletives and slam the room door. Once the elevator closed, Ashley let out the biggest sigh and started to cry. Tears streamed down her face. As she held onto the handrail, she began to shake as she released all of the fear and stress of what had just happened in the hotel room.

She replayed all of the events of the night over and over in her mind on the ride home. *How could he ever get the idea that I would spend the night in a hotel room with him?* she wondered.

Retrieving a spare key from the battery compartment of a flameless candle on her porch, Ashley was finally home. Ditching the fancy outfit, she took a hot shower, scrubbing her skin until the water turned cold. She then brushed her teeth, gargled with mouthwash, put on comfy pajamas, and crawled into bed with her journal.

Tonight, she wasn't writing to herself. Tonight she was writing to Alice.

*Oh, Alice, I wish you were here. I need you so much right now. Something went horribly wrong on a date tonight. It was fun. Well, it was kind of fun and kind of awkward. One minute, I felt like a princess, and the next, I felt like a piece of meat being desired by a hungry animal. I don't know what I did wrong to make him think he could touch me like that. He had his hands all over me, and I hated it.*

*Alice, he even led me to believe I wanted it because I said I would make it up to him. I only meant I would have coffee with him or go to lunch. Since when does it ever mean what he thought?*

*If you can help me, Alice, I would appreciate it. Help me understand what I did wrong. Should I have known he was like that? Do I need to learn how to talk to men? Did my dress give him the idea that he could touch me? I know I didn't intentionally send out those signals.*

*Maybe it was him. Maybe he is just like that with all the girls. I need guidance, Alice. Send me a sign somehow, will you? I never want to be in that situation again. I know you will guide me. I trust you, even though you are not here. I feel you sometimes. I know you are here, somehow, in some way.*

*Good night, Alice.*
*p.s. I feel better already. Thanks.*

# Calming the Storm Within

For two straight weeks following the disastrous date with Brian, Ashley tuned out the world and focused on gaining her self-esteem back. She felt foolish for believing he had good intentions in taking her out. When in reality, he treated her as if she owed him for his indulgent evening on the town.

The next morning, Ashley woke up at 4 am and went for a run. She desperately needed to figure out what went wrong with Brian. Going over that night in her mind made her skin feel like spiders were walking up her arms. Thinking about him arranging that night in the hotel, what he was thinking about the whole time they drove to the city, while they ate dinner, while he was running his fingers up and down her arm- the thought nauseated her. Running was the perfect distraction for processing her thoughts.

In her usual manner, she spoke positive affirmations and told herself she would work this out, fix what was wrong, and make Alice and Dr. Brown proud. Nothing was going to get in her way of succeeding. There was something to learn in the experience, but she had yet to figure out what that was.

By some great miracle, Ashley did not cross paths with Brian at the office. Each night on her drive home, she thought about Alice and silently thanked her for this miracle. After a week of not running into him, he was out of her mind, or so she thought.

Sunlight filled Ashley's bedroom, waking her for the day. It was Saturday, and the outdoors beckoned her attention. Rising early to get the lawn mowed, she was happy to connect with nature. Chores were a delight after the stressful two weeks.

Opening the back door, she took a deep breath of the outside air, closed her eyes, and exhaled every thought, every worry, and every fear. Smiling at herself as she walked along the brick walkway to the shed, she remembered when she first arrived at Alice's. She remembered the emotional turmoil she was in and how much these bricks bothered her. She smiled because she could see how far she had come. She no longer despised doing the yard work; she enjoyed it. She no longer struggled with the stone wall around her heart; she was allowing her heart to feel things, and most of the time it felt good.

For hours, she worked in the yard cutting back spent flowers, pulling weeds, trimming bushes, edging, and mowing. She was sweeping up the driveway when she heard the familiar sound rumbling down the street. A smile graced her face as her heart picked up an extra beat at the thought of Greg. She walked to the street to meet him when he pulled up.

"Good morning," said the mailman.

"Good morning," Ashley replied, followed by "I thought you were Greg."

"No ma'am, Greg is going to be out indefinitely. He's got some medical issues."

"Oh no! What's wrong with him?" Ashley asked.

"Ma'am, I'm not at liberty to discuss his personal matters."

"Please, sir, if you could just tell me how I can get in touch with him?" Ashley pleaded with a despairing look on her face.

The mailman looked her in the eyes and offered, "PO Box 100 here in town. Address it to

Greg Harper. The postmaster himself is delivering the cards to Greg."

"Oh, thank you so much. Can I ask one more question? What happened to him? Sir, Greg, and I are friends. We talked just a few weeks ago about the lady who lived here before I did. He knew Alice very well."

"Ma'am, I've already told you more than I should." He said, then paused and looked at her, "Cancer, he has cancer. Good day."

The truck pulled away, leaving Ashley standing there in shock. Tears fell from her eyes as she walked back to the house and sat on the porch swing. She was numb, remembering being curled up under Greg's arm on the swing one night, not too long ago.

*Did he know then? He must have. He must've known. He never said anything. Oh…* Ashley began to cry as she thought about these things. Rocking on the swing, she thought about how fragile life is. She thought about all the people she had lost. Then she remembered Alice. She remembered how many people Alice had lost as well.

*Wait, Greg isn't dead.* She snapped out of her dreary thoughts, popped off the swing, and got back to work. *I need to stay focused.* She told herself as she finished putting away the gardening tools.

A shower and some clean clothes, and Ashley was off to run errands. Greg did not leave her mind; however, she thought about what she would say to him. She figured the words would come once she got the card and sat down to write in it.

Her car was full from shopping, but she was in no hurry to carry the bags in, so she brought a few in and put them away. Before returning to the car for more, she heard a familiar voice.

"I got the last of them for you," he said as he carried in six bags at once.

"David! What a surprise. Thank you so much!" Taking some from his hands, they both went into the kitchen.

"I figured you didn't see me when you pulled into the driveway since the sun was shining in your face. I was standing in the street talking to the contractor. Figured I'd come say hello."

"I didn't see you at all. I'm glad you're here. How's the house coming along? I see it is going up pretty quickly."

"Yes, they say they'll make the original date. That's not usually the case with new house construction, but I paid good money to get the job done. I should be moving in by the end of October."

"Two months and we'll be neighbors, imagine that," Ashley said, as she nodded her head with a smile.

They chatted and caught up on life while David handed her the groceries to put away.

"Any plans for the holiday weekend, Ashley?" he asked.

"Plans? No. I hadn't even considered it. But now that you mention it, I do have a long weekend."

"David, I'm gonna fix something for dinner, and I'd love it if you could stay. Can you?"

"Ashley, I would love that," he said with a satisfying smile. "I have been on the road so much over the last several weeks, take-out food is getting sickening. Thanks for the offer. I gladly accept. What can I do to help?"

"Can you make a salad?"

"Absolutely! Just give me a bowl and a cutting board, I already saw the vegetables, and I see the knife right here," he said as he reached for a knife in the block on the counter.

Without skipping a beat, Ashley pulled out pots and pans and began setting them on the stove; one with water, one with a little olive oil in it. Next, she started chopping up garlic and onions and tossed them into the oil. In a mixing bowl, she crafted meatballs with freshly chopped herbs, salt and pepper, and Parmesan cheese. Those went into a deep skillet with a glass lid on the stove. She prepared garlic bread with butter and fresh garlic and held off toasting it until the meal was ready.

David had the salad beautifully made when she was done setting the table.

"There! Is there anything else?" David asked as he placed the salad bowl on the table.

"I think we are all set with the food. I'm going to fix us some nice drinks."

"I don't drink," David said regrettably.

"Oh, David, no worries. I don't either. I'm gonna make us something fruity." She replied as she carried watermelon, strawberries, and blueberries from the fridge, and frosted glasses from the freezer. Ashley put fruit-flavored seltzer water and a splash of unsweetened grape juice in each, popped in a couple of straws, and handed one to David, which he held up to toast to the evening.

"To a home-cooked meal," he said.

"To friends," she replied.

They clinked their glasses together and enjoyed the refreshment.

"Let's sit outside while the meatballs and sauce cook," Ashley suggested.

Sitting on the steps, looking across at David's house, they sat in silence for a few minutes. Ashley was purely content and relaxed.

"So would you like to go on an adventure with me for the holiday weekend since you have no plans?" David asked.

"An adventure?" she replied.

"My family has a yacht and I'd like to take you out on it," David replied.

Ashley choked on her drink. She stood and excused herself and walked into the house. Suddenly, a panic swept over her. *Why does everyone want to get me alone... In a hotel... On a boat... Why is this happening? What am I doing wrong?*

Ashley stirred the sauce and then the meatballs. David approached her and asked, "Are you all right?"

Ashley didn't reply. She was struggling with what to say. Flashbacks of the restaurant with Brian were flashing in her mind. *Did I unknowingly invite David here to have the same thing happen? Is he…*

"Ashley?" David said as he touched her arm.

Smacking his hand away, Ashley exclaimed, "Don't touch me!"

David stepped back in shock and stood silently.

Looking at him, realizing David was not Brian, Ashley turned to face him and said, "I'm sorry."

She began to cry as she tried to finish explaining. Covering her eyes with her hands to wipe the tears and squeeze the bad thoughts out of her head, she dropped her hands, looked at David, and said, "I had a bad experience."

David interrupted her before she could finish, "Ashley. It's OK, I'm not that guy. I'm not gonna touch you again. I'm not gonna hurt you. And I don't want to take you out on the yacht alone. That's not what this is about."

Looking at his face, trying to assess his sincerity, Ashley remained silent. A few tears slipped down the side of her nose. David handed her a tissue from the box on the counter. He continued to be completely honest, "It was my dad's idea. He called me and told me about all the things you've been doing. He told me how you've advanced in your job, that you've registered for full-time evening classes at the university, and that you have been managing the house wonderfully. He is very impressed with you. He said he is proud of you." David paused to see if she had anything to say.

"He told you all of that?"

"Yes. He wanted to know if I would be willing to take you out on the yacht for a little vacation before you start working and going to school full-time. He thought it would be a nice break for you and a nice treat. I've never seen him this thrilled about someone's progress before."

When Ashley heard those words "about someone's progress," she remembered that she was Dr. Brown's charity case. That everything she had was in part due to his generosity, along with Alice's. This only made her feel worse. Turning around to stir the sauce again, Ashley was overwhelmed with all of this.

"David, will you watch the food? I need to step aside to be alone for a minute."

Without waiting for his answer, she walked to Alice's bedroom and shut the door. Sitting on her bed with both feet on the floor, Ashley dropped her face into her hands and began to cry. *Alice, I need you. I don't know what to do. I'm not ready for this. I need more time. I need to figure out what went wrong with Brian before I fall into the same situation with someone else.*

She looked up from her tear-soaked hands and saw Alice's journal. There were pages she hadn't read. Maybe there would be wise words. Maybe there would be something she could use. Wiping her hands on her shorts, she picked up the journal and opened it to a random page.

*Dear Lord,*

*I have many things stirring trouble in my mind. It is more than I can bear. Your word tells me that "more than the sounds of many waters, than the mighty breakers of the sea, the Lord on high is mighty." I come to you, this mighty one, and ask that you calm the storm in me. Please, Lord, let it be that I might see you and know peace in my soul. You are my rock, my fortress in the storm. Amen.*

Stunned at what she just read, Ashley opened the drawer on the nightstand, looking for a

pen. Finding one, she wrote in the margin, Ashley –
David – yacht, and then marked the date. She
closed the journal, bowed her head, and said, "Let it
be for me," and she set the journal on the
nightstand and went back to the kitchen.

With a smile on her face, she walked up to
David, looked him straight in the eyes, and said, "I
trust you. I would love to go on the yacht with you.
Can you tell me more about it?"

Smiling back at Ashley and looking deep
into her eyes, he replied, "I would love to tell you
more. How about we talk over dinner? The
spaghetti is ready, and so is the garlic bread."

Ashley looked at the table and saw
everything waiting for them, then looked back at
David and said, "You are amazing. Let's eat."

# Beautiful Surrender

*I don't know anymore who I'm writing to. First, I thought it was Alice. Then I thought I was writing to myself. But now I feel some strange desire to write to the same God Alice did in her journals. I don't know who that is, though I know her God answers her prayers. I'm proof of that. But how do I pray to a God I don't know?*

*Things in my head are so messed up. I have too much to try and figure out. I used to talk to Alice every day. She always helped me, and now I am unsure of some pretty important questions. I need answers. I want to get past this stuff. I don't just want to deal with it for the rest of my life. I really want to claim victory over these tormenting thoughts, if that's even possible. I hope it is.*

*Well, whoever you are, I'm just gonna write out my thoughts without trying to make sense of them. If you're able to read them or hear my thoughts…how would I know anyway? Well, I'm gonna pretend you can. I'm just gonna write to Alice's God.*

*I'm really messed up inside my head. Lots of crazy stuff went on in my life before I ever came to live at Alice's. But so much has gotten better. I have made so many improvements in my life. I am proud of myself, but still I know what lies beneath the appearance of my progress. This torment in my mind has me losing my grip. It was obvious to me tonight when I smacked David's hand away after he simply asked me what was wrong. That right there was a lightbulb moment for me, and I don't know what to do to change my thinking. Will I ever be able to appreciate the attention of a man ever again?*

*Tonight, when I read Alice's journal, she asked you to calm the storm in her, and she quoted a verse about the mighty breaker of the sea. She called you her rock and fortress in the storm. She was crying out to you just as I am right now. Oh God, is it any coincidence that David asked me to go out on the ocean in a boat? This is so overwhelming to me. Everything that I fear is in front of me, and yet I hide it from everyone. I told David I would go with him, but I am terrified on the inside.*

*If everything else that has been told to me about you is true, and I mean from the beginning, if you are really the God who hears and answers prayer…well…then I want her God to be my God. Will you help me? Will you calm the storm in me, too?*

Ashley closed the journal and fell asleep, crying in full surrender.

Days later, Ashley had just finished packing for her trip with David when the doorbell rang. David was right on time. Opening the door, she greeted him with a cheerful smile.

"Good morning, Ashley."

"Good morning. Come on in. I think I am all ready to go. Just need to check the locks and timers."

"Great. These bags over here, are they all set to go in the truck?"

"Yes, but I can carry them."

David was out the door with her bags before she returned from checking the back door.

Within minutes, they were on the road heading towards the ocean for their Labor Day weekend escape. On the way, they agreed that talking about work was forbidden for the next three days. They challenged each other to find only positive things to talk about for their mini vacation. They stopped to get breakfast at a little diner just before getting on the highway. When Ashley ordered scrambled eggs, home fries, with rye toast, and an iced coffee, David simply said, "Make that two. I'll have what she's having."

Back on the road, they took turns scanning the radio stations for songs they could sing along to. David wasn't shy about singing, and Ashley was thrilled. She never mentioned it, she just sang along to the songs with David. They had natural chemistry in everything they did.

Stepping out of the truck, David inhaled the salty air and said, "You smell that?"

Hesitantly, Ashley replied, "It smells kind of fishy."

"You'll get used to it, plus it's not as fishy once you get out to sea."

David strapped all of the bags over his shoulder and picked up a smaller one when Ashley protested, "David, I can take my bags."

"Follow me, Miss," he replied, ignoring her objection, and headed for the boat.

Once all aboard and introductions were made, the group set sail. Ashley watched as the land slowly disappeared. David didn't bother her much at first, knowing she would need time to adjust and to soak in all of the beauty.

*There's something special about watching the only connection to your world slip away from you. You find yourself left with only what's inside you and what is around you.* Ashley thought.

Walking up next to her, David asked, "How are you feeling? Queasy at all?"

"No, not at all. This is quite breathtaking and thought-taking for that matter."

"Being out here does have a way of freeing your mind," David replied

"David, can I ask you a personal question?"

"Of course you can."

"When you pray before we eat, do you pray to the same God that Alice prayed to?"

Turning to face Ashley and looking compassionately as he smiled, he replied, "Yes, Ashley, Alice, and I believe in the same God."

She remained silent and looked out across the golden sea. Her mind began drawing up comparisons between David and Alice. Thankfully, David didn't ask her if she believed. She wasn't sure how she would have answered. It seemed David never crossed the line on subjects when Ashley dipped into tender topics. Ashley found comfort in talking to David.

"Hey guys, we're going snorkeling soon. Do you wanna join us?" Natalie and Bella asked as they approached David and Ashley

David looked at Ashley and asked, "Want to give it a try?"

Ashley looked at the excitement on the girls' faces and replied, "Absolutely!"

They whisked Ashley off to get into their swimsuits, gave her a quick rundown of how to snorkel, and assured her it would be fun. Soon after, they were in the water exploring. Then they ventured off onto the island for another round of exploration.

When evening fell upon them, they enjoyed a meal together on the boat. At one point, Ashley drifted off in her thoughts, realizing how wonderful this day had been. There was no fear, not even about being in a bikini in front of David. It occurred to her that she never gave her appearance one thought the entire day. She never felt anyone looking at her body or flirting with her. With this realization, she began to think that maybe she didn't do anything wrong on her date with Brian. Maybe it wasn't about what she was wearing or what she said. A sweeping sense of relief came over her. Then she caught herself and returned to the conversation at the table.

After dinner, each went their way on the yacht and found a place to relax for the evening. David and Ashley put on sweatshirts and sat outside looking up at the stars. David asked, "Are you enjoying the trip so far?"

"I am, more than I can put into words."

Then silence settled between them. Once again, Ashley felt a warm sensation inside her. It felt like an embrace, yet no one was touching her. She gazed up at the sky, looked at the moon, and in her mind, she thanked God. In that moment, a shooting star sailed across the sky. Another wave of emotion rushed over her, and a tear rolled down her face. She remembered her words last weekend to the God who answers prayers. She knew he heard her words and answered them.

Ashley turned her head, looked at David, placed her hand on his, and said, "Thank you for everything."

She held his gaze for a long while. The light from the moon illuminated his face, and then he opened his arms, inviting her in for a hug. Without hesitating, Ashley curled up under his arms and

rested her head against his chest. All of her prayers
were answered.

# Beautiful Innocence

Upon waking to the smell of coffee and bacon, Ashley opened her eyes and took a deep breath, inhaling the delicious aromas. She was not used to waking up to the smell of food already prepared. Taking a moment to appreciate all that was good, she drew the covers up to her chin and hugged them. Hearing her stomach growl, she popped up out of bed, put on some shoes, and ventured off to the kitchen.

"Good morning. Sleep well?" Jeremy asked as he poured pancake batter on the griddle.

"The best sleep ever," Ashley replied as she poured herself a cup of coffee.

"There she is," Natalie announced as she entered the kitchen.

"Sleepyhead is awake," Bella chimed in.

"What time is it?" Ashley questioned.

"It doesn't matter, we're just fooling with you," Bella replied.

"The sun's been up for hours, though," said Natalie.

"I smelled bacon!" David exclaimed as he made his way to the coffee pot. He was followed by the rest of the crew.

"Jeremy puts the *gourmet* in breakfast. Wait till you taste the scrambled eggs," Skip commented.

"And I bet you've never had mint chocolate chip pancakes before, made with fresh mint leaves. And he makes his own special chocolate drizzle syrup just for these pancakes. They're so delicious." Kate added.

"You guys have my mouth watering," Ashley replied.

Each one filled their plates and gathered in the dining area to eat together, and even Jeremy sat with them. He was an expert at having all of the food ready so everyone could eat at the same time.

"This is my kind of vacation," said Peter.

"The kind with the very best of everything in one place. No traffic, no credit cards, no miserable people," he continued.

"Just friends," he said, as he lifted his glass for a toast.

"To friends, old and new," Jeremy added, as he clinked his glass to Ashley's. Then they all lifted their glasses and saluted "to friends."

Leaning into Ashley, as to speak only to her, David asked, "Would you like to go on a little adventure with me?"

"Sure, what'd you have in mind?"

"I thought we could take the jet skis out and go to the beach when we get near the island."

"That sounds great. I need a few minutes to clean up and get changed. Meet you back up top in about 45 minutes," Ashley replied.

"Perfect. See you soon," David finished, as they both exited.

Once fitted with lifejackets, David showed Ashley how to drive the jet ski. They practiced near the boat before going out further. Once Ashley was comfortable with the power of the watercraft and David was confident in her ability to control it, they headed out.

"This is so much fun," Ashley shouted, as they rode the waves.

At one point, David spotted some whales and signaled Ashley to stop. He pulled up next to her, and they turned off their engines. They watched the whales put on a show in the distance.

"This is amazing. We're out here with the whales," Ashley said, and watched in complete astonishment.

When the whales swam away, David and Ashley continued toward the island until they finally reached the shore and landed the jet skis on the beach. In an unguarded moment, Ashley removed her lifejacket and ran over to David, jumped on him, and repeated, "Thank you, thank you, thank you, thank you, thank you. This is the best time of my life."

David caught her and swirled on his feet from her impact. Ashley hugged his face by wrapping her arms around his head, completely caught up in gratitude. Then she jumped off of him and lay down on the sand on her back.

"I'm in heaven," she declared.

David's face was beaming with joy. He sat down next to her until she grabbed his arm and pulled him down next to her.

"Look at that," she said, as she pointed, "not a cloud in the sky."

Still smiling, David simply absorbed her energy.

Rolling onto her stomach to face him, she propped her chin on her hands and began a string of questions.

"Do you do this every year?" Ashley asked.

"Go out on the yacht? Yes," he replied. "Have this much fun? No."

"What do you mean, no?" she asked.

"I'm not usually this adventurous," he answered.

"But you seem so good at it," she replied.

"I know how to do these things, but I just haven't done them in a long time," David responded.

"Why not?"

Lifting his head to look her in the eyes, he answered, "Because I haven't wanted to until now."

"What changed your mind?" she inquired.

"You," David answered.

"Me?" Ashley questioned.

"Ashley, from the day I met you, I've noticed a beautiful innocence about you. You're unaffected by the ways of life. You're not weighed down by all of the injustices in the world. You face heavy burdens with a light spirit. I don't know how you do it. If I faced all that you have, I just don't know what I would do or how I would handle it."

"Wow, I never imagined you saw me that way," she replied.

"You have such a vibrant energy about you. It makes me want a piece of it. I want to know what it's like, so I feed off of your excitement. Ashley, you make me feel alive again," David confessed.

"Well, good! I'm glad you're not dead. I've had enough of that."

Rising to her feet, she turned and grabbed his hand, pulling him up to his feet. Then she turned and ran with him in tow into the water. Diving in, she swam out as far as she could with one breath. When she came up to breathe, David was already there.

"Wow, you're fast," she said.

Then she lay back and floated with her eyes closed. David just looked at her shining in the sun. Then he got an idea and dove down to the sand to pick up a starfish he saw. He placed it on her stomach.

"Aaaaahhhhhh!!! What is that?" she screamed as she sat up.

Treading water, she saw the starfish sink to the bottom. While David was laughing, Ashley splashed him and swam over to him in an attempt to push him under. He simply lifted her out of the water by her hips and tossed her a few feet away. They played like this until they both grew tired.

As they walked back to the shore, David grabbed a bag from the jet ski. He came prepared with sunscreen and snacks. They sat looking out over the water in silence after rehydrating and having a bite to eat.

"I'm gonna take a little nap, hope you don't mind. I'm wiped." Ashley said, as she rolled onto her stomach and set her face down in her arm.

"No problem. I'll be here when you wake up," David answered.

As Ashley closed her eyes, she thought about God. She smiled, knowing he was indeed answering her prayers. She was enjoying the company of a man, and it was truly beautiful. It seemed so natural, no fear, no pressure, no awkwardness. Ashley felt loved by God and it was enough.

# One Day at a Time

The whirlwind of emotions storming through Ashley after her weekend with David had her seeking to understand once again what she wanted in life. It seemed that once her prayer was answered, it caused her to question her desire in the first place.

*Is this what I really want? I didn't expect it to be like this*, she thought. For Ashley, the questions stirring in her mind were causing quite a storm of confusion.

*Why does life have to happen so fast?* she wondered.

Tuesday, following Labor Day, Ashley welcomed the stress of being back at work as she knew it would take her mind off of herself. She also started full-time evening classes that week. She had no idea how it was all going to work out, but she was determined to take advantage of the scholarship Dr. Brown had given her. Honoring Alice was always at the forefront of her mind.

In the blink of an eye, the week had gone by. Only when Ashley woke up on Saturday morning did she realize it was the weekend. Shocked as she was when she saw 10 a.m. on the clock, she was also relieved to have caught up on some sleep.

Walking to the kitchen to pour a glass of juice, she saw the mailman walking up to the door. Opening it before he reached the doorbell, she said, "Good morning."

He returned the greeting and handed her a small box. "Special delivery," he said. Then he walked away, telling her to have a good day.

Curiously, she looked at the box and noticed it had no postmark on it, no address either, just her name written in blue ink. She brought it inside and sat in Alice's chair, just looking at the box. Then she slid her finger under the flap to break the seal and slowly opened the package. A folded piece of paper lay on top of white tissue paper. She took the folded paper without looking under the tissue paper and read the handwritten note.

*Dearest Ashley,*

*I received your card, and my heart melted. I am so touched that you kept pressing George to find a way to get your message to me. He told me when he came to see me. He said he saw something genuine in your eyes. I told him how glad I was that he trusted you.*

*I know you expected me to call since you gave me your phone number, but I am just too sick right now. This is not easy to go through. Every day, I think about how peaceful that day was with you and how there was not a care in the world for either of us in those moments we spent together. I want you to think of me not here like this, in all of this pain, but as I was before you ever talked to me. I've enclosed a video of me performing some of my songs. Yes, I am a singer and a songwriter too. These video clips are from the past year, so they are recent. One day, I hope to return to the stage and sing again.*

*Thank you for caring about me, Ashley. My thoughts of you have been rays of sunshine throughout my treatment.*

*Blessings, Greg*

Streams of tears ran down Ashley's face as she read the letter. She couldn't even look in the box, for her emotions had overtaken her. She cried hard for Greg. Leaving the box and the note on the table, she went to the bathroom to let it all out. She cried and screamed out to God. Dropping to her knees in front of the tub, Ashley prayed for Greg from the depths of her heart.

"As you have delivered me from my darkest hour, God, please deliver Greg. Please heal him and give him comfort through this treatment. Oh God, please," she cried.

Falling face down to the floor, Ashley curled up in a ball on the bathroom rug. She hummed a soft tune to comfort herself. When she was calm, she returned to the living room.

Taking her laptop out of the travel bag, she placed it on the kitchen counter and plugged it in. Taking a deep breath, she put the disc in and hit play. There he was, full screen, standing on stage in a club with only an orange glowing light around him. He sang a ballad with his eyes closed most of the time. His voice was delicate and tender, and he sang with deep conviction. Standing in the kitchen, Ashley could feel his emotions as he sang and she was mesmerized.

Feeling weak in the knees, she took the laptop to the couch and watched the entire video. He sang beautiful songs. When it was over, she closed the laptop and went outside to the porch swing where they had sat together. She tried to blend the Greg in the video with the Greg she knew from the day they hung out. She rocked on the swing and felt his warm embrace as if he were right there that night.

Honk! Honk! sounded from the street, snapping her out of her tender thoughts. Looking across the yard, she saw David waving as he pulled into her driveway, stopping at the top. He yelled down the driveway from his driver's side window, "Are you gonna be around for a while?"

To which she replied, "Yes," with a hearty shout. He waved and backed out of the driveway and continued down the road.

Ashley took that as a sign that she needed to get on with her day. After skipping yard work last weekend, there was much to do. She grabbed a quick breakfast and got straight to cutting the lawn.

As she passed by the gardens bordering Alice's yard, memories flooded her thoughts, not only of Alice but of Greg. Even so, as she neared the front yard, closest to the street, she saw David's house all finished on the outside with workers hammering away inside. She thought, *You're gonna be my neighbor very soon.* Then her memories of the fun they had on the yacht flashed through her mind. She was smiling ear to ear as she finished mowing the grass.

With trimmers and yard waste bags, Ashley worked meticulously around the shrubs and cut back the spent perennials, deadheading some flowers until she filled six bags. Dragging each one to the front side of the fence, she heard her stomach declare its need for food. Looking around at her completed work, she noticed how vibrant the colors were in Alice's gardens. Remembering the journals, she realized once again that Alice spent a lifetime building this masterpiece, and she felt blessed to be able to witness the remarkable beauty.

Pulling off her gardening gloves, Ashley headed to the shed to put the tools away. Just then, she heard a truck in the driveway close to the garage. Within seconds, David was around back with his arms full and a smile as wide as Texas on his face.

"Hungry?" he asked.

"Yes. How did you know? I'm starving!" she replied with a growl in her stomach.

David set the food down on the picnic table in the backyard. He had thought of everything, including drinks.

"Wow, fresh cut fruit, pasta salad, and what's this?"

David opened up a foil pouch, revealing piping hot vegetable shish-kebabs.

"This is amazing!" declared Ashley.

"Last weekend was the best time I've ever had in my life. It left me with a whirlwind of emotions. I'm not sure what to do with them, so, like I said, I welcome the distraction of school and work," she continued.

David remained silent as he was noticeably thinking about what she meant. Then he asked, "If you had the best time of your life, wouldn't it be reasonable to think that you would like to do it again or at the very least do something similar, you know, with me?"

"It would be reasonable to think that. And I would like to spend more time with you. It's just that I am trying to understand where I fit into all of this. Where do I fit into my own life? Alice gave unselfishly to me, everything that was hers, from her heart to her home. Your father gave selflessly of his fortune and his kindness. You have given to me."

David cut her off by saying, "I gave you of myself, Ashley. I gave you me."

"I know you did. You still are. But I cannot always be the recipient of everyone's generosity. I must figure out how I can participate in my own life.

I need to find out what I have to offer. I need to be able to give back."

"No one is expecting…" David couldn't finish his sentence because Ashley chimed in.

"I know you don't expect anything in return for your kindness. I guess what I meant to say was that I need to find me. I have just been going through the motions, doing what was asked of me. I've been blessed by all the experiences, but I need to know who I am. What do I want out of life? What is my contribution to the world? That is what's stirring in me."

"That's impressive," David replied.

"What is?"

"The fact that you can see through all of this so deeply and that it matters to you. It speaks volumes to your character and integrity. It's very deep, Ashley. You even have me thinking now."

"David, there's more. Do you know Greg, the mailman?" Ashley asked.

"Vaguely, why?"

Ashley proceeded to tell the whole story about Greg, even about the time they spent together that one day. When she told him about the video and the note, it left David speechless.

"You see, it's even more complicated than you thought. There is still more that is on my mind about last weekend that I haven't even had time to process. Life is happening so fast. I'm spinning inside."

"I had no idea there were so many things going on in your life," David replied.

Noticing David's shift in demeanor, Ashley continued, "Don't forget what I said at the beginning of this meal. I had the best time of my life with you last weekend. That is something I know I want in my life, David. I like having you in my life. This right now is more precious to me than… Well, it's just precious. That's all. You always know what I need, when I need it, and you always give it to me. I wonder how you know these things. That is part of what's swirling in my mind, too. I like you. I'm just not sure what to do with that or any of these things in my life. Now that I am super busy with work and school, I guess it will just have to evolve on its own."

"One day at a time is a good principle to live by," David replied. Then he smiled and lifted his water bottle to hers. "To one day at a time," they said in harmony.

# Hope is Alive

Frozen and unable to move, a power so strong left Ashley stuck in her bed. Lying there wide awake, she felt numb, heavy, and empty all at the same time.

What is this? She wondered. Trying to figure out what was making her feel like this, she ran a list through her mind:

1. *I'm not sick*
2. *I'm safe*
3. *I have a job*
4. *I'm going to school*
5. *I have a home*
6. *I have food*
7. *I even have a dog now*
8. *I have friends*
9. *I know I'm happy*
10. *I even have God now*

*What on earth is going on? Why can't I get out of bed?*

Rolling over, she acknowledged her body was not hurt. She lay there in bed with the sun shining through the window, and the stray dog, which showed up yesterday, on the floor next to the bed. Ashley had no desire to rise and face the day. That is, until the dog began barking and pointing towards the door, then she had no choice but to let her out.

While opening the door to let the dog out, Ashley picked up the Sunday newspaper from the mat. It occurred to her that the dog, still unnamed, could run off at any time. She figured, *it came on its own—it can leave on its own.* The dog seemed loyal, though, and interested in staying. Ashley couldn't figure out why.

Ashley thought about the dog as well as the other things that she had a hard time understanding. "Maybe I'm supposed to just think today. It seems that's all I feel like doing," Ashley told the dog as she headed to the living room to sit for a while. Bending over the sides of Alice's chair to get the fuzzy blanket, Ashley noticed her iPod under the table.

I haven't seen this in a while she said as she unplugged it from the charger. Snuggling down in the chair with the blanket, she popped her feet up on the ottoman and put the earbuds in to listen. *It has been so long since I listened to this,* she thought.

She simply hit shuffle and then play to allow the random assortment of songs to play. Each song seemed to send a message to Ashley. One girl was singing about moving on and finding someone new. Another song was about the tragedies in life and how they leave us feeling empty. Another song was about a best friend, and then it hit her as she thought about Greg and David. She thought that she would like to do something nice for Greg, but also with David.

She took the earbuds out and contemplated, *What can I do for Greg?*

He had written again and said he would be done with treatment by the beginning of November and then back to work soon after that.

David, on the other hand, was moving into his newly constructed house in November. Then all of a sudden, Ashley got a grand idea, *I'm gonna make a Thanksgiving dinner for us—me, David and Greg, and whoever they might think to invite.*

The idea warmed her heart. The more she thought about it, the more she realized that they could all build on their friendships.

Ashley rested in the thought and returned the music to her ears. Then it happened just like it did last winter. The music swept over and through her so powerfully that it caused her to cry. She didn't even understand why she was crying. She tried to figure it out. She let the music move her as she listened to the words. Then turned it off, searching deep inside her, looking around for clues. What is it? What is going on with me?

Getting up from the chair, Ashley went to her room to get her prayer notebook. Then she sat on the bed and began to write to God.

*I don't know what is going on. Are you trying to tell me something because I am not hearing you? I have no desire to go running like I usually do to work out these feelings. I am trying to think, but I've got nothing. Tell me what you want me to know.*

She sat there with pen in hand and just waited for God to speak to her.

*I have a purpose,* were the next words she wrote.

Looking down at the words on the paper, she read them aloud, "I have a purpose."

Then she spoke out loud as if to God.

"I know I have a purpose. I have to take care of Alice's house and work to show Dr. Brown I appreciate all that he's done for me."

She was quiet again. Listening. *That's not it? There's a greater purpose?* she questioned as if she was responding to God.

"Well, what is it?" she replied.

*"The answer is inside me?"*

Ashley grew frustrated and blurted out, "Just tell me what it is!"

Just then, her doorbell rang, snapping her back to the present moment. She folded the notebook and went to the door. Opening it, she found three teenage girls standing on her porch.

"Hi. What can I do for you?" she asked them.

"Ma'am, we're looking for donations to help our…" one girl started to say.

"…sick mom," another girl finished.

"Yeah, she's got cancer, and we have no food," the third girl chimed in.

Suddenly, Ashley felt old and wise and saw right through their attempts at getting money. She remembered all that she had learned and came up with a plan instantly.

"Why don't you girls come in for a few minutes? I'll fix you a snack. Sound good?" she asked them.

"OK," all three said at once.

They followed Ashley into the kitchen and were greeted by a dog.

"What's his name?" asked one of the girls.

"It's a she, and I don't know her name."

"Isn't it your dog?"

"No, she's not. She showed up here not long ago. They don't have room at the animal shelter, so I'm keeping her for a little while."

"Oh, that's so nice of you. You should give her a name," said one of the girls.

"But if she already has a name, won't she be confused?" Ashley asked the girls as she popped cinnamon rolls into the oven.

"No, any name you give her is better than leaving her a nobody," replied one of the girls.

That hit Ashley like a punch in the heart. She stopped fixing the snack and realized that she had been spending every day and night with a dog with no name.

"What should I name her? Do you girls have any ideas?"

"Hope," said one girl.

"Yeah. She came to you, hoping you would take her in, right?"

"Yeah, she's hoping to find a home. You should name her Hope."

Stunned that these girls came up with the name, especially since Ashley had just written to Greg about hope, she looked at the dog and then at the girls, and seeing a greater scenario playing out before her eyes, she agreed to name the dog Hope.

Ashley squatted down to feed the dog, rubbed her belly, and tried out her new name.

"Do you like that, girl? Do you like getting your belly rubbed, Hope?"

She looked at the girls, and they were all smiling and petting the dog, too.

The timer went off, and the smell of warm cinnamon buns filled the room. When Ashley set them on the table, she asked the girls their names as they each took a bun.

Ashley managed to get the girls to fess up to the truth about why they were looking for donations. She discovered that the girls were running away from home and realized they had no money. So they came up with their idea of collecting for their sick mom.

When Ashley related to them that she completely understood where they're coming from, the girls opened up even more personally; each one told their story. Ashley knew what she had to do. There was no doubt in her mind about what her purpose in this moment was.

She decided to let the girls spend the rest of the day with her, and then they could all sleep in the living room for the night. Ashley was determined to convince these girls to go back home, but she also wanted them to know they could always come to her anytime for help with anything.

The girls played with Hope outside and even did a little yard work willingly on their own. They noticed sticks and branches had fallen, and they offered to pick them up. When it came time for dinner, all the girls offered to help Ashley, and she let them. Each girl had some part in preparing the meal and setting the table.

Ashley told the girls that by morning, they would all have to return home when she left for work. It was part of the deal she made with them for the future endeavors with Hope or even future times at the house with Ashley. The girls felt such a strong connection to Ashley; the idea of getting to be with her and Hope again made them want to return home just so that they could come back.

Ashley returned to her bedroom around midnight and opened her prayer notebook. She wrote these words before closing her eyes to sleep, *"to be a beacon of hope for the next generation."*

# A Greater Purpose

The hustle and bustle of November was upon Ashley as she began planning for Thanksgiving. David had already moved into his new house across the street. Greg had finished his cancer treatments. The teenage girls had decided not to run away, and Hope, the stray dog, was still sleeping next to Ashley's bed on the floor each night. Life was beginning to make sense for the first time to Ashley. She had a good idea of her purpose in life, and it energized her to believe this was her calling. Knowing she couldn't do anything in life without trusting God, she made sure to start and finish each day with him.

*Dear God, thank you for bringing me to another day. I have no idea what will be, but I know you do. Please use me to make a difference today. I'm so thankful you saved me and made me a better person.*

Dialing David's cell, she was on a mission to ask him what his plans were for the holiday. The brief call ended with an invitation to breakfast at his house. Grabbing her notes, she slipped on her sneakers and went across the street to David's house.

"You've made this new house feel like a home, David. It's got such a warm feel to it. How did you do that?" Ashley asked as David poured coffee into the cup she was holding.

Smiling, David replied, "I'm glad you felt what I was hoping to achieve by blending some old stuff with new. I had copies of most of the pictures that were lost in the fire. I had them framed in antique frames. I also pulled lots of family heirlooms from storage and brought all of my old furniture from my apartment. This eclectic mix, along with the earth tones, makes the house feel like an old home. Of course, the floorboards make a huge impact since they are from an old home renovation project. Recycled wood gives this house its original charm."

David had whipped up a beautiful breakfast and was serving Ashley as he was speaking. Grabbing his cup of coffee, he joined her, gave thanks, and they both enjoyed the meal together.

"You asked about Thanksgiving. Did you have something in mind?" David asked.

"I do. That is, if you don't already have plans. Do you?"

"I do not."

"I would like to have Thanksgiving together with you and invite people who could use some encouragement. I was thinking of inviting Greg and a guest if he has one, the girls who've been visiting me, and I don't know if you have anyone to invite. I feel strongly about all of us getting together. What do you think?"

"I love it!" David replied without hesitation.

"So, tell me about these girls," David requested.

Ashley proceeded to explain how they showed up at her door and how their friendships have grown over the weeks. As she was speaking, more ideas popped into her mind.

"You know, David, I just got an idea. I think it would be eye-opening for these girls to volunteer at the soup kitchen, the food bank, and the animal shelter. They would learn so much, and it would do wonders for their perspectives on life all around. I'm gonna check into it and see what I can do."

"I believe you're starting to see the bigger picture, Ashley, one my father saw many years ago."

When David said that, it seemed a lightbulb went on in Ashley's mind, and she began making the connections. Holding the cup of coffee to her lips, she stared out across the living room and thought about all that she had learned from the generous acts of kindness of others.

Snapping out of it, she said, "Let's plan on a late afternoon Thanksgiving dinner so the girls can be with their families and come here afterward. I'll stress the importance of family and encourage them to enjoy all that they have. How about we ask them over for 4 o'clock?"

"That sounds great. That will give Greg time to get ready if he can make it, and that gives me time to help out at the shelter," David answered.

"The shelter?" questioned Ashley.

"I volunteer to serve food on Thanksgiving to the homeless people downtown. It's a family tradition. So 4 o'clock works perfectly for me."

"Do they need more volunteers? I'd like to serve." Ashley asked.

"Of course they do. I'd love to bring you down there." David's eyes almost shed a tear, but he controlled his emotions and carried on with the conversation.

"Well, I am so full of ideas and excitement, I'm gonna go home and get things done. I will get back in touch with you with details," Ashley said as she headed for the door.

"Are you going to ask Greg or should I?" David asked.

Pausing in thought for a moment, she replied, "I'll ask him. I have his number. I'll tell him we're doing this together and offer him the opportunity to bring something. He will feel better about joining us if he is not just a guest."

"Good call. Thanks for thinking of all of this. Have a good day, Ashley," David said as he held the door open for her.

A few days later, after giving thought and prayer to her plans for Thanksgiving, Ashley called Greg.

In a choked-up voice, Greg responded to her invitation. "You caught me off guard with this, Ashley. I don't have plans because I wasn't sure if I would be alive. I don't have any family either."

Ashley heard a sniffle and listened as Greg talked emotionally about his life. She felt his pain. She knew his pain. She also knew what he needed to feel better.

"Greg, listen. I understand where you're at. Do you like to cook? Can you make mashed potatoes?" Ashley asked.

Coughing to clear his throat, Greg replied, "Yes, I know how to make mashed potatoes."

"Great! Can you make them for our dinner on Thanksgiving? David and I are volunteering at the shelter, and it would be a big help if you could help out with our meal. Will you join us?"

"Of course I will," he answered.

They talked some more, and Greg offered to bring more items. Later in the week, David called Greg and offered him the use of his house to prepare the food while they were at the shelter. Greg agreed. The plans were coming together smoothly.

Ashley also placed calls to the parents of each of the girls. Once she shared her intentions with the parents and explained that it was important for the girls to come on their own, they understood. They agreed not to persuade or prevent the girls from having dinner at David's house on Thanksgiving. The parents were grateful for Ashley's mentoring them and told her they noticed a change in their daughters. This brought tears to

Ashley's eyes, and she immediately went to her prayer notebook.

*My heart is full, Lord. I see your hand in all that I do, and I am continually in awe. None of this would be happening without you. I can't imagine living a single day without you. Without you, I was nothing. You have made me into something and given me a purpose. Please bless all those involved over the next couple of weeks as we prepare for our very first Thanksgiving dinner together. I love you.*

The morning sun had broken through the curtains and woke Ashley up early. Hope was already looking at her, fully awake and ready to go outside.

"This is it, girl. This is the big day. Move over so I can kneel and pray."

Dropping to her knees and leaning on the bed, Ashley spoke her prayers.

"All that I am is in you, Lord. Make me a blessing. Might I see you in every face at the shelter, show compassion, and greet each one with a smile? I pray for Greg that he would feel well enough to eat and strong enough to have fun. Oh Lord, may your light shine on all of us today, in Jesus' name, Amen."

"Come on, let's go greet the sun," Ashley said to the dog.

Opening the door, Ashley found a basket of flowers and goodies sitting on her doormat. Looking around to see who might have just delivered it and seeing no one, she carried it into the house, while Hope ran outside. After setting it on the counter, she found the card.

*Many bountiful blessings to you, dearest Ashley. Warm regards, Dr. Brown.*

Pressing the card to her heart, Ashley closed her eyes and gave thanks. Then she heard a knock at the door. Opening it again, she was greeted by the girls holding a cup of coffee and a small box of breakfast treats.

"Oh, girls, thank you so much. Do you want to come in?" she asked.

"No, we can't. We just wanted to give you something to start your day. Thank you for helping to feed the homeless. That's nice of you," one of them said.

"See you later," one shouted as they walked down the driveway.

"4 o'clock across the street. See ya!" said another one.

Once again, Ashley's heart swelled. She gave thanks again. Then she walked over to David's with the basket of treats to share. Hope came with her this time. Looking around at the yard as she walked down the driveway, she noticed the way the girls had kept things nice and tidy. It made Ashley proud. It wasn't long ago that she was the one helping Alice with the yard, and already she is in the position to help others. *Amazing*, she thought.

When she arrived at David's, she was surprised to see Greg already there. The house smelled of pumpkin pie. The table had stacks of folded linens on it, along with autumn decorations.

"Hi! Boy, you guys are at it already. What is all of this?" Ashley asked as she pointed to the table.

"David told me he didn't have any decorations, so I picked up a few. You said the teenage girls were coming, and I thought they would like it. Feel like decorating?" Greg answered.

"Well, alrighty then. I'll get right on it. What time do we have to leave, David?" Ashley asked.

"10 o'clock."

The three of them worked together, talking and preparing food. They would have time to cook after they served food downtown, but the preparations would be done ahead of time. Greg agreed to stay at David's to keep an eye on some of the food that took longer to cook. He also looked forward to the football game on TV.

While Ashley and David were at the shelter, Dr. Brown arrived at the house. Greg remembered him just as Dr. Brown remembered Greg. They both agreed it would be a big surprise for both Ashley and David when they returned home. Dr. Brown shared stories with Greg. They also had a great time watching the game, both avid football fans, opposing teams though.

Ashley cried in the car on the drive home after serving the homeless. It was all too close to home for her. She felt very blessed to have been taken under the wings of Alice and Dr. Brown. David understood her emotions and just let her cry it out. He knew she just needed to release the pressure inside her. They were both all smiles when they pulled into the driveway. Seeing the extra car, David knew whose it was.

"Get ready to meet my dad, he's here," David told Ashley.

"Really?" she asked.

"Oh, this is amazing. I might just burst with happiness," she continued.

Smiles and hugs for everyone as they entered the house. It felt like a real home to Ashley. She tried with all her might not to break down in tears again. She didn't.

They spent time catching up while Greg resumed control of the kitchen. Just before 4 pm, the girls arrived, each with a gift in their hands-flowers for Ashley, a pie, and a plate of cookies to share.

After the introductions were made, everyone started setting the table. Each brought food out and placed it along the center of the table. Ashley stepped back for a moment to take it all in. She stood there, smiling, and watched how everyone worked so well together. Then she caught David watching her. He smiled and winked at her. She smiled and continued gathering things for the table.

Greg was feeling a bit tired, so he took a seat first, and Dr. Brown joined him. The girls noticed three chairs in a row along one side of the table and claimed them as theirs. The one chair that remained empty next to Dr. Brown had a single flower placed on the plate. Everyone knew it was in memory of Alice.

As David brought out the platter and set it at the center of the table, Ashley lit the candles, and she and David took the remaining seats, one at each end. David and his father, in unison, reached out for the hands of their neighbors, and everyone followed suit. Dr. Brown, being the elder, began the prayer and asked each one to offer up a prayer of thanks before eating. So, around the table, each one did and ended with Ashley.

It truly was a miracle for all of these individuals to be gathered around one table in a house that had once burned down. There is a power so great to defy the odds placed against you; you only need to believe.

# From the Author
*Original note from 2016*

This concludes the story of Ashley. Use your imagination and all that you've learned about her to decide where her life takes her from here. I may come back and continue her tale, but for now, this is the end. I believe she has learned more lessons in these last few months than some of us have in a lifetime.

If there's one thing I want you to take away from Ashley's story, it's that you have a choice to believe in yourself, in God, in the good of others, or nothing at all. I've tried to illustrate my faith through this character. Many of her situations were relatable to me. Many of her thoughts were mine. I have grown as I brought Ashley through the crucible into a blessed life. I pray for all who read the story from beginning to end, to give it a try with all your heart. I believe. I pray you do as well.

# Journal Prompts

# Reflecting on "The Sound of Beauty"

The opening scene is a real situation that occurred to me during the most difficult season of my adult life when I chose to stay in the basement of a nearby unoccupied house during the winter of 2014/2015.

There was no heat and I had only a Keurig, a lamp, and a cell phone. I slept under a pile of blankets while fully dressed in my winter coat and hat. Many days were spent processing all that was going on in my life.

It was during this time that I heard about a new singer through social media and began watching his YouTube videos on my phone. Though I never had the same dreams that Ashley had, I did wish for *more*. For me, it was *peace* that I longed for.

During this season of my life, I started writing poetry. I wrote about anything and everything that crossed my mind. You see, at that house, I was safe. I was able to use my creativity to work out emotional trauma. The poems that I wrote while there are published in my book "Released To The Wild" by Lori Minutoli.

It was also there that I wrote this story. I created the word, Kaleidastorm, from kaleidoscope and storm. When we look through a kaleidoscope, we see beautiful art formed from broken pieces of colored glass and objects. In this storm I was determined to make something beautiful of my life. "Beauty in the storms of life" is what Kaleidastorm means.

Over 400 poems in one book, and this entire story came out of that horrible season of my life.

I hope you are inspired to see beauty in your "broken pieces." Your life has meaning and purpose; you just need to find it.

Write whatever came to your mind after reading "The Sound of Beauty."

# Reflecting on "The Dream"

Sometimes life feels like a nightmare, and when it does, it's difficult to focus on anything but survival. In "The Dream," Ashley survives a nightmare by entering into another dream, one she created from her deepest desires. When she wakes up from that dream, she is confronted with the harsh reality of her surroundings: a cold, dark basement. But there is hope when the nice neighbor arrives with warm muffins. This act of kindness is a reminder that there are people out there who care.

When I wrote this chapter, I did not know I was writing from my deepest desires. I thought I was creating a story for people to read. It was later, I realized that I wanted some of what Ashley wanted: normalcy. And many years later, I, too, had a dream, or a vision, of what my future could look like. I believed it to be possible. I am currently living proof that my beautiful dreams are coming true. That is the context of my latest published book, "Tucked In Flowers- Hidden in Plain Sight" by Lori Kirkland.

Write what came to your mind as you read "The Dream." Even if it seems ludicrous now, just write it.  Someday, you may look back or simply remember these were your thoughts, and you'll see how things worked out for you.  Additionally, by writing it, deeper truths may be revealed. Sometimes, you just need to open the door to possibilities and allow them to enter.

# Reflecting on "The Plan"

Sometimes, no matter how hard you try to do the right thing, things go wrong. In this chapter, Ashley pushed herself to create the life she had always dreamed of. She took action. She did the mental work, the physical work, and got a job.

When the house burned down, it could have been the end of everything for her. Alice seemed to be an angel sent to help Ashley. What I hope you realize as you read this story is that there is a deeper story inside each character's role. That's how it is in real life, too. The world doesn't revolve around just one person. We are all interconnected and play a role in many others' lives. A simple "Hello" to a stranger could change the course of their day.

As you get to know Alice, you will see the depth and scope of a genuinely good soul. I hope she also inspires you to do good in this world, to be the light in someone's dark world. It doesn't take much, just a willingness to do something.

Write what came to your mind as you read "The Plan."

# Reflecting on "Emerging"

Even though I wrote this, as I read it ten years later, I am deeply moved by the things Ashley is learning and growing to understand. The thing is, she is allowing herself to feel all of her emotions. That is an important step in personal growth. Take time to go back and reread the parts of this chapter that make you feel something. Pause, and come back here, and write what that is. Continue through the chapter. Don't worry if it makes sense, this is for you! Just write what you feel. Let yourself emerge into something even more beautiful. Express yourself in any way you feel moved to.

# Reflecting on "Beauty Prevails"

Only by living do we learn how to live. When we make it through a storm, we are then better prepared for the next one. The more storms we survive, the more we learn to make provisions long before a storm hits. Nature teaches us that it is even possible to thrive after a natural disaster. Ashley faces yet another devastating storm.

Write about a time in your life when you thought it was impossible to get through a particular storm. When the worst possible thing happened, what was it, and then, write what came of it. Over time, did you learn from it? Are you prepared for similar storms now that you've survived that one?

It has been ten years since I was in that basement, living practically homeless. I have learned a tremendous amount of survival skills since then. I also know how to prepare myself or prevent myself from ever being in that situation again. I often have to remind myself that there is "the other side" of the storm- the beautiful side: the rainbow, the blue sky, the blooming flowers, the regrowth, the healing, the thriving.

In this chapter, we also witness the kind, loving, and caring ways Dr. Brown and his son take care of people. These are further examples of beauty in the storms of life. Take time to reflect and write all that comes to mind as you read this chapter. What you write will be your survival road map.

# Reflecting on "Always Remember"

As a gardener, I can tell you the significance of every plant in my yard. One of my favorite stories to tell is about when my daughter was maybe 5 years old. She pulled up a tree sprout from near the doghouse in our back yard and then asked me if she could plant it somewhere to watch it grow into a tree.  I agreed. We planted the sprout in the front yard. It turned out to be a great Silver Maple.

In this chapter, we heard the story of the first plants Alice and Henry planted in their yard. While reading the journals, Ashley came to understand the value in keeping memories alive by not only writing them down but also by talking about them.

Write what came to mind as you read this chapter.  Can you relate? Does it inspire you to create journals like Alice did?  The answers to these questions are for you to self-reflect. There are no right or wrong answers.

# Reflecting on "A Beautiful Mess"

Write what came to your mind as you read this chapter. Write your predictions about the three different men who have become of interest to Ashley. Can you relate to a time when more than one person was interested in you? Or even a time when you were interested in more than one person? Write your thoughts and see where this takes you.

# Reflecting on "Dream Date"

Thinking about all the work Ashley has been doing on herself, think about how that work helped her make the decisions she did in this chapter. Write what's going through your mind after reading "Dream Date."

# Reflecting on "Calming the Storm Within"

Ashley has learned to power through difficult situations, or as I call them, storms. She is determined to achieve all that she sets her mind to, all that was in her dream. In this chapter, we see how she calms the storm within her and the beautiful outcome it produces. My hope is that you will also practice being honest with yourself, trusting yourself, and pressing on towards the things you've set your mind to achieve.

Write what came to your mind as you read "Calming the Storm Within."

# Reflecting on "Beautiful Surrender"

Have you ever noticed that there comes a time when you reach what seems to be the end of yourself, the end of your abilities, whether it's physical or emotional? When you've done all the steps you were taught, said and did all the things you were supposed to, and still you ended up feeling overwhelmed or defeated? I have. When that time came, I had nowhere and no one to turn to.  I thought *there has to be something bigger than me that has the power to change things.* That's when I cried out to God, just like Ashley did. It was Alice's faith that had inspired Ashley to believe.

Write what came to your mind as you read "Beautiful Surrender." Maybe it's not God that you have cried out to, but if you can relate, please write it here.  If you are at the end of your abilities right now and you have no one left to turn to, maybe this is the moment you call out to Alice's God. There are no right or wrong ways to make the connection. Please, write what's on your mind.

# Reflecting on "Beautiful Innocence"

When we are free to be ourselves, without fear of judgment, and fully trust the people around us, it allows a childlike abandonment to come out. Ashley feels completely safe in David's presence, and it shows. Have you ever felt that way?

Ashley also acknowledges God in this beautiful experience she is having. Write the thoughts that came to your mind as you read "Beautiful Innocence."

# Reflecting on "One Day at a Time"

Healing isn't linear; it's cyclical. Ten years after first writing this story, I am just now understanding this concept. I've always believed healing to be a straight path with bumps along the road. You know, fall down seven times, get up eight. It doesn't mean you've fallen back; it means it's time to put what you've learned into practice, again. Growth is healing on repeat.

Ashley recently had a wonderful time with David and felt that God had answered her prayer. Everything should be smooth now, right? Now that she has developed a connection to God, she has a way to deal with everything. She can just pray about it, and it will all work out, right?

Yet here she is with her thoughts spinning until David reminds her to take things one day at a time. We do that, don't we? Think too far ahead. Worry about things that haven't happened yet. This is where we need to reflect on the cyclical habit of putting good practices into action. We need to slow down, breathe, and focus on what's good. When we live in the now of our day, and remember what we aim to achieve, it keeps our vision clear.

Take time to breathe and focus on what you want to achieve in your life. Write it down; from the smallest achievement to major life goals, or whatever came to your mind as you read this chapter. You will always be able to come back here to check your progress.

# Reflecting on "Hope is Alive"

When an unsettled feeling sweeps over you, what do you do? Shake it off? Distract yourself from thinking about it? Tell someone?

Ashley learned to sit in it. Yes, she used her journal to write through it, but she sat through the unsettledness and just listened. Who was she listening to? Let's just stay neutral and say she was listening to her inner voice. Have you ever done that?

Write what came to your mind as you read this chapter. If nothing, leave it blank. Maybe the next time you pick up this book, you will have something to write. Maybe you can reread the chapter with the intention of listening to your inner voice. Whatever crosses your mind, write it.

# Reflecting on "A Greater Purpose"

When we are in survival mode, we often cannot think outside of our own trauma. Ashley learned how to navigate the healing process through the kindness and care extended to her by others. Her experiences come full circle when she offers the same kindness to the people she's grown to care about. Ashley attributes her understanding of having a greater purpose to God.

Take time to search yourself to discover your greater purpose, something that reaches beyond you. Remember, the world doesn't revolve around just you. We are all connected and play a role in each other's lives. What do you hope to discover? What to want your purpose to be?

I have thought back to this final scene many times over the last ten years. It is still a dream of mine to this day, to have these experiences. I am a work in progress as the healing cycle continues.

Write what came to mind as you read "A Greater Purpose."

# In Conclusion

Just as I wrote this story, to imagine a life I wanted to live, take time to write yours. Today, it may only be a story, but in the future, it may become your real life.

Write your final thoughts on this book. I ask you to do that because, over time, your thoughts will change. If you've taken the time to write responses to each chapter, this will be the summation of all of your thoughts. Maybe, you will come to a deeper understanding of who you are or what you want out of life. Maybe, you are considering talking to God, or writing to him, even if you don't know who he is or don't believe God exists. This is the place to write those thoughts.

# One Final Note

If you've arrived on this page and you've participated in the journal writing, *thank you.* That is the entire reason I republished this book- to engage with the reader. Ten years have passed since I first wrote the Kaleidastorm story. It was originally written in 2015 as a short story series for Channillo- a subscription-based digital publishing platform. Back then, people were skeptical about paying online to read my stories. They asked me to print them so they could read them. I decided to do so as a book.

Once my divorce was finalized in 2016, I found great strength and motivation from the lessons Ashley learned in this story. Even though I wrote it, I had no way of knowing then that my actual life would turn out similar to Ashley's. I didn't live the same experiences, but the life lessons she learned, I have benefited from in real life. I often wonder how on earth I had the wisdom to write such things. Each time I read the story, I resonate with a different part of Ashley's journey.

The Kaleidastorm story ends on Thanksgiving, and this tenth anniversary edition,

*Finding Beauty Within*, is being released in November 2025 to symbolize my life's journey coming to the same place. It's not the end, however, only the beautiful beginning.

This is my second self-published book as Lori Kirkland. To hear the story of how I became Mrs. Kirkland, check out my poetry book, "Tucked in Flowers- Hidden in Plain Sight," available on my website: lori-kirkland.com, along with links to all of my other books.

Please feel free to email me or write me a handwritten letter to let me know your thoughts on this book, the journal writing process, or feedback in general.

Lori Kirkland
285 Columbus Ave
Pawtucket RI 02861

lorikirkland11@gmail.com

# About the Author

Lori Kirkland is the author of ten self-published books, including poetry, inspiration, and romance fiction. She enjoys reading, writing, and going on adventures. She is the founder of Pawtucket Poetry, where she hosts poetry open-mic events and supports poets globally on Instagram.

Lori lives in Pawtucket, Rhode Island, with her husband Craig, a multi-talented poet, artist, and filmmaker from Jamaica.